"DOES THE THOUGHT OF SEX BEFORE DINNER OFFEND YOU, MR. BOYD?"

"Sex at any time is a great idea," I told her.

She kicked off her shoes, reached behind her back and unzipped her dress. When it dropped around her ankles, she kicked it away. Her black mini-slip floated after her dress like some fragile magic carpet. Then she turned to me, put her hands on her hips, and bared her teeth in a tigerish smile. Her lacy black stockings were self-supporting; a minimal pair of lacy white briefs clung tight to her hips, and a lacy black bra contained the almost horizontal thrust of her breasts. The alternate black and white effect was wholly erotic.

In what seemed no time at all she was standing in front of me naked, except for the lacy black stockings. I grabbed her into my arms and she came willingly, pressing her body and thighs fiercely against mine.

"Why, Mr. Boyd." Her voice was a caress.

"Under the circumstances," I said, "don't you think you could call me Danny?"

"I couldn't do that, Mr. Boyd," she murmured. "My social position only allows me that kind of familiarity with bellhops!"

"Your social position is about to become horizontal," I told her, carrying her purposefully to the bed. . . .

SIGNET Thrillers by Carter Brown

- [ ] CATCH ME A PHOENIX (#Q5910—95¢)
- [ ] CHINESE DONAVAN (#Y7122—$1.25)
- [ ] A CORPSE FOR CHRISTMAS (#Q6153—95¢)
- [ ] THE CORPSE (#Q6468—95¢)
- [ ] THE DAME (#Q6402—95¢)
- [ ] THE DEADLY KITTEN (#Y7152—$1.25)
- [ ] THE DESIRED (#Q5985—95¢)
- [ ] DONAVAN (#Q6033—95¢)
- [ ] THE DREAM MERCHANT (#Y7031—$1.25)
- [ ] THE EARLY BOYD (#Q6321—95¢)
- [ ] HAD I BUT GROANED (#Y7222—$1.25)
- [ ] THE HAMMER OF THOR (#Q6496—95¢)
- [ ] THE IRON MAIDEN (#Q6425—95¢)
- [ ] NEGATIVE IN BLUE (#Q6220—95¢)
- [ ] NIGHT WHEELER (#Q6103—95¢)
- [ ] NUDE WITH A VIEW (#Q6068—95¢)
- [ ] THE PIPES ARE CALLING (#Y7182—$1.25)
- [ ] SO MOVE THE BODY! (#T5704—75¢)
- [ ] SO WHAT KILLED THE VAMPIRE? (#Y6549—$1.25)
- [ ] THE STAR-CROSSED LOVER (#Q5940—95¢)
- [ ] WHO KILLED DR. SEX? (#T5744—75¢)

THE NEW AMERICAN LIBRARY, INC.,
P.O. Box 999, Bergenfield, New Jersey 07621

Please send me the SIGNET BOOKS I have checked above. I am enclosing $_____(check or money order—no currency or C.O.D.'s). Please include the list price plus 35¢ a copy to cover handling and mailing costs. (Prices and numbers are subject to change without notice.)

Name_____

Address_____

City_____State_____Zip Code_____

Allow at least 4 weeks for delivery

The Mini-Murders

by
CARTER BROWN

A SIGNET BOOK
NEW AMERICAN LIBRARY
TIMES MIRROR
in association with Horwitz Publications

Published by
THE NEW AMERICAN LIBRARY
OF CANADA LIMITED

© Copyright 1968 by Horwitz Publications, a Division of Horwitz Group Books Pty. Ltd., (Hong Kong Branch), Hong Kong, B.C.C.

All rights reserved. Reproduction in part or in whole in any language expressly forbidden in any part of the world without the written consent of Horwitz Publications.

Published by arrangement with Alan G. Yates

First Signet Printing, December, 1976

123456789

SIGNET TRADEMARK REG. U.S. PAT. OFF. AND FOREIGN COUNTRIES
REGISTERED TRADEMARK — MARCA REGISTRADA
HECHO EN WINNIPEG, CANADA

Signet, Signet Classics, Mentor, Plume and Meridian Books are published in Canada by The New American Library of Canada Limited, Scarborough, Ontario.

PRINTED IN CANADA

COVER PRINTED IN U.S.A.

Chapter ONE

I turned around and stared openmouthed at the vision resplendent that suddenly confronted me, then finally realized that beneath all that black and silver lurked a human soul. A guy in his early twenties with carefully cropped hair that looked as if it had been sprayed with stardust, and guileless blue eyes. He was wearing a black silk shirt open all the way down to the navel, and a pair of skintight black pants that looked as though they had been specially designed to throw his crotch into spectacular relief. Around his middle was a wide black belt with an enormous silver buckle. There was a chunky silver medallion around his neck.

"Mr. Boyd?" His voice was someplace in the treble range and slightly off-key.

"Sure," I nodded. "I'm Danny Boyd."

"Flavian Eldridge." He smiled brilliantly. "Mr. Freidel's personal assistant. I have a car waiting outside."

"I figured maybe you flew in all by yourself." I looked at him in wonder. "What with that bird of paradise outfit you're wearing, and all."

He preened a little. "It is a marvelous outfit, isn't it? You know something? Dion personally designed it for me."

"He must have a great sense of humor," I grunted.

"Oh?" His smile was real bland. "Did he say something amusing when he called you long distance?"

We went out of the airport to the car—an imported German aristocrat with a white paint-job—the kind that has that cute gunsight on the hood to help your aim when you're hunting Californian pedestrians. I stashed my bag in the trunk, then climbed into the passenger seat beside Eldridge, feeling a little happier now the sartorial nightmare would be hidden inside the car.

As we drove through the center of the town I noticed Santo Bahia hadn't changed very much since the last time I was there. It was still the same swank coastal resort town, and all the olde worlde shoppes had their windows jammed tight with the kind of antiques that would have made Martha Washington itch to borrow her husband's ax. A right turn, about a couple of miles out of town, took us away from the coastline, and a second turn five minutes later put us onto a dirt track which looked like it headed straight into a dense forest of Monterey pines.

"So Freidel lives in a tree?" I inquired.

"Not exactly, Mr. Boyd." The vision beside me smiled tolerantly. "It's just that Dion values privacy above everything. Without it, he simply couldn't create." His long lashes fluttered provocatively at me. "I'm just dying to ask, but I suppose I shouldn't. I mean, just what does Dion want from a tough sophisticated New York private detective like you?"

"It's a good question," I admitted. "I'll be intrigued to hear his answer."

"Oh!" He pouted unhappily. "It's all to be a great big secret, is it? I thought he might have told you something when he called last night."

"Just that he wanted me out here today, and the fee he offered was fat enough to get me onto the plane this morning."

"Perhaps it's all the silly vandalism that's been plaguing us lately." He concentrated for a few moments on navigating a narrow wooden bridge that was humpbacked, like road engineering had gone out of style. "I've told him a hundred times already, it has to be one of the house models. They're three jealous little bitches, and if he fired the lot of them it would immediately resolve the problem." His deep sigh was compounded with overtones of despair. "I must say, Dion can be so frightfully obstinate at times!"

The car rounded a sharp bend and came to a stop about a hundred yards farther on, in front of a pair of massive iron gates. A uniformed guard walked across, gave me a hard professional stare, then nodded at the driver.

"How's everything with you, Sam?" Eldridge simpered.

The guard's mouth tightened. "Just fine," he said curtly. "I'll open up the gates for you."

"What a wonderful physical specimen Sam is," Eldridge said admiringly, as he watched the back of the departing guard. "I don't know why, but that marvelous muscular type of man is always so noncommunicative. Whenever I stop for some chitchat, he just walks away."

"Maybe the power of your intellect makes him speechless," I suggested.

"Do you honestly think so?" His face brightened. "It hadn't occurred to me before. Next time, I'll try and think up some topic of mutual interest before I approach him."

"How about women?" I said, straight-faced.

A winding driveway led toward an enormous three-story building that looked like some demented architect's idea of a French chateau, stolen from a television rerun of an old Charles Boyer movie. Adjacent to the house was a giant-sized pool, with people dotted around it and—at that distance—they looked like a miniature advertisement for the good life.

"Freidel has some kind of a persecution complex?" I wondered out loud. "Gates, guards, and an electrified fence. What is he scared of? An invasion from Outer Space, or the boys from Internal Revenue?"

"It's like I told you, Mr. Boyd. Dion values his privacy. Besides, if he made it easy for anyone to steal his designs, he'd be out of business inside a month."

Eldridge parked in front of the house and we got out of the car, then walked up the imposing wide stone stairs to the front door.

"Sims, the butler, will take care of your baggage," he said casually. "Dion was most insistent I bring you straight to him the moment we arrived."

The butler proved he was real by opening the front door just as we reached the top stair. For a moment there I figured he must be psychic, then realized there would obviously be a phone hook-up between the guard at the gates and the house. The front hall was a slightly scaled-down version of the concourse at the old Grand Central, with doors opening off it about every place you looked. An elegant circular staircase swept up to the second floor, sporting a gold-and-white balustrade.

"Dion uses this floor for his creative work," Eldridge said, "the second floor for living, and the top for sleeping. You'll find it's like living in an institution for the more insane of both sexes, but I expect you'll get used to it. Most people do, eventually." He opened a door and stood to one side to allow me to enter first. "This is Dion's main workroom."

I walked past him into the kind of fantasy I sincerely hoped was just the workaday world of a fashion designer. The room itself was drab, containing a couple of full-length mirrors on one wall, a battered outsize workbench cluttered with pieces of material and other junk, and a few straight-backed chairs scattered around. What sent the adrenalin pounding through the Boyd veins and arteries, and caused a minimal flurry in the nether regions, was the kind of company a fashion designer kept.

Standing on a chair was a tall statuesque dark-haired girl wearing a bored look and an ankle-length dress that was almost totally transparent. Looking at her standing against the light, I could see that all she was wearing beneath it was a scrappy pair of white briefs. She stood patiently while the fashion designer hacked away at the hem with a pair of shears. Leaning against the wall was a lissome redhead in the smallest swimsuit I had ever seen—and what there was of it was full of holes, so that hardly anything was left hidden. I wondered vaguely why she bothered and what the fishes thought of it. Standing real close to me was a small blonde, exquisitely plump in the right places, in only a bra that was doing its best to contain the superb plunge of her boobs and white briefs that made a delicious contrast to her deep golden tan. She had a real smug look on her face, as if she knew she was the Sultan's choice on today's menu-card.

The fashion designer stepped back from the chair and slowly nodded his approval. "I guess that's about it, honey," he announced in a vigorous bass. "You can get down now."

"I can't," she said flatly. "I'm pinned too tight all the way down the back."

"Uh, Dion?" Eldridge cleared his throat nervously. "I have Mr. Boyd with me."

"Later," the designer snapped.

The blonde turned toward me and gave me a sultry smile as she ran her hands down over her rounded hips. Then she took a long deep breath that almost lifted her breasts straight out of the cups of her bra, giving me a glimpse of a small slice of pink aureoles. Her nipples strained eagerly against the flimsy material. "Hi, Mr. Boyd," she said throatily. "I'm Kitty."

"And I'm Deborah," the redhead said from across the room. She shifted, and more holes seemed to appear in her swimsuit. "You know what they say about redheads, Mr. Boyd. They're much more fun, more talented—like, active."

"Will the both of you clam up and let me concentrate?" Freidel snarled, then gestured impatiently to the girl on the chair. "Get down, will you?"

The brunette extended one leg a few inches until the material of her dress stretched taut over her thigh. She hesitated for a moment, looking down at the floor, then shrugged helplessly. "So I'll jump," she muttered. A moment later she made the fatal error of shifting her weight toward the edge of the chair. She let out a startled yelp as the chair tipped suddenly and pitched her face-forward onto the floor; then, as she scrambled wildly back onto her feet, there was a sharp ripping sound. The tight dress gently dissolved from around her torso like an early morning heat haze, until it finally lay in a soft heap around her ankles. That left her wearing just her scrappy briefs, along the top of which was a fringe of black hair. Beneath them the gentle contours of her crotch were dark-shaded. Her breasts were small but nicely rounded. Her dark-pink nipples were extended. I nodded approvingly.

"Stephanie!" Freidel's voice was outraged. "What are you, anyway? Some kind of a clumsy female-type cow?"

"I warned you, Dion," she said in a tight voice. "You're lucky I didn't do myself an injury."

"Get the hell out of here before I do you a permanent injury someplace unspeakable, you lame-brained clotheshorse!" He gestured wildly. "All of you—get the hell out!"

The brunette shrugged disdainfully, then headed for the door. Her briefs hung low on her buttocks, which bounced provocatively as she walked. As I watched them with lascivious intent, I felt a gentle pressure on my elbow.

" 'Bye, Mr. Boyd," the blonde gurgled. "See you later." The big baby-blue eyes looked wide and innocent. "If you think Stephanie looks skinny now, wait until you've had the chance to make a closer comparison with my statistics."

As she walked past me, I got the full impact of what she had just said from her rear view. Her bottom was superb. Her briefs clung nonchalantly to the smooth white orbs that quivered rhythmically as she went on toward the door. Then I felt another gentle pressure on my elbow.

"The name is Deborah," the redhead said in a cool voice. "I'm the one who's built just right, Mr. Boyd. Neither skinny nor fat. And remember what I told you about redheads, if you didn't already know. When the fire burns, it really burns."

"I'll remember," I assured her, peering in through the holes in her swimsuit. Then I turned my head a fraction to give her the full benefit of the left profile— the ultimate creative achievement of my parents—but she didn't faint in ecstasy the way I had expected.

"Most men get a nervous twitch when I'm around," she said in a consoling voice. "But don't worry, Mr. Boyd. I know a wonderfully original way of curing it."

If I looked closely enough, I could see her rump in all its glory, trace the cleavage between the high curved cheeks from top to bottom. As she headed out of the room, I saw that it rolled more than bounced, in a gentle grinding motion. My eyes glazed with misery as I thought of all the years I'd wasted as a private detective when I could have been a fashion designer, making models.

"I've just wasted about three goddamned hours on that creation!" Freidel grinned reluctantly as he came toward me. "You'd figure there has to be some way of making Stephanie hold still."

"Maybe you could buy her a chastity belt," I suggested. "Then throw away the key."

He didn't jibe with my idea of how a male fashion designer should look at all. Freidel was a big guy someplace in his late thirties, and built like a pro footballer with most all of the beef still muscle. His thick black hair made a crown of tight-curled ringlets on top of his head that was matched by the luxuriant growth on his upper lip. The dark eyes were set deep in the satanic-looking face and seemed to have an inbuilt gleam of derision. I wondered what he did for fun and got the nasty feeling it probably had something to do with blood sports.

"I'm glad you made it from New York so fast." His handshake was firm. "It's Danny, isn't it? We don't go much on formality around here."

"That, I'll believe," I told him, "and it's Danny. What kind of problem have you got that needs expensive little me so fast?"

"Right now I'm not too sure if I have a real problem, or if it's only greasy kid's stuff. Either way, I can't afford to take any chances." He looked pointedly at Eldridge. "Don't you have to go powder your nose or something?"

"Oh, very well!" Eldridge looked like he was about to stamp his foot or something equally dramatic. "But if this means you include me among your suspects, Dion, you must be out of your tiny mind. Fire all three of those stupid little bitches and that will be the end of it."

"Out!" Freidel said in a brisk voice.

Eldridge flounced out of the room with his head held high, looking like a martyr determined to die bravely when he met the firing squad waiting in the front hall.

"He should have made that, four stupid little bitches, including himself," Freidel grinned.

"You keep talking to him this way and maybe he'll stop wearing that outfit you personally designed for him," I said wistfully.

"Ridiculous little fag. I don't know why I bother."

"Leave us talk about something different before my stomach quits on me," I pleaded.

"Maybe I should give you some background first." Freidel turned, moved the crumpled transparent dress Stephanie had been wearing out of the way with a vicious kick, then perched on the edge of the workbench. "Sit down, Danny. You can't make yourself comfortable in this room, but you can take the weight off your feet."

"I was sitting too long in that goddamned plane," I told him.

"All this"—he made a grandiose all-embracing gesture with his right arm—"is the heart of the Freidel creative empire. Harry Kempton, my partner, looks after the business side, the bulk manufacturing and distribution. I guess Flavian told you I also eat, sleep, and live here. It gives me both privacy and security. At least, it did up until recently."

He brushed each side of his flowing moustache with a slow ritualistic movement of his index finger. "I'm about to show my spring collection; we're into the last-minute panic of altering designs, fittings, and late inspirations. Then, to drive me out of my brilliant mind, we discover we've got some kind of psychotic cut-up lurking in the woodwork! Someone's been deliberately sabotaging the new collection during the last few days."

"What happened exactly?" I queried.

"The first thing was when Lenore Brophy—my ace cutter—walked into her workroom one morning and found the evening gown she'd been working on the previous day had been hacked into small pieces. It happened to be the most elaborate design in the whole collection. The next day, Deborah discovered someone had poured acid over four or five of the new model swimsuits. Just yesterday, we found a couple of lengths of a very special material we need for the collection had also been cut to pieces. Luckily the supplier still had some in stock and could air-freight immediately, but it could have been very different."

"So you called me," I said. "Why me?"

"You've got a reputation around Santo Bahia for getting results." He grinned momentarily. "Even if certain people don't like the way you go about it."

"The way you've got this place surrounded, with that electrified fence and guards at the gates," I said, "I guess it figures it must be one of your staff."

"It's more complicated than that," he growled. "I asked some influential people down here to stay until after the showing, so the house is kind of crowded at the moment. You've already met my staff with the exception of my cutter, Lenore Brophy. I figured you don't need to worry about the domestic staff because they're never allowed into this part of the house at any time. But I'm not sure you can rule out the guests the same way."

"How many guests?"

"Five, including my partner, Harry Kempton. I can't see him as a suspect exactly, unless he's suddenly flipped without me noticing. There's Libby Cathcart, a Manhattan socialite who also writes a column for one of the top fashion magazines. Polly Peridot"—the derisive gleam in his eyes brightened for a moment—"the dowager darling of the jet set! Then Art Luman, and his associate, Chuck Reilly, make up the balance."

"What does Luman do?"

"Invest his money at great profit to himself, mostly. Confidentially, he has an interest in the Freidel operation, too. But Harry and I never talk about that in public because Art's image outside of finance is slob, mostly!"

"If he's a kind of silent partner, I guess we can leave him off the list of suspects along with Kempton," I said.

He paused maybe a half-second too long before he answered. "I guess so. Maybe it would be better if you make your own judgments as you go along, Danny."

"What are you doing to prevent any more sabotage?"

"At the end of the working day everything goes into a locked room, and I'm the only one who has a key." He held up his hand to stop any protest before I made it. "The only alternative is to get a bank vault built into the house, but I don't have either the time or the money for that crap."

"Do you suspect anybody in particular of the sabotage?" I asked, without being real hopeful.

"Flavian's sure it has to be one of the house models, but that's the kind of inbuilt reaction you'd figure from him. He doesn't have any proof, or any motivation even, except he's sure they're all psychotic little bitches."

"And, like you said, he makes four. How about him as a prime suspect?"

Freidel shook his head slowly. "I don't see it, Danny. He figures I'm the genius in the fashion field—and he's right, naturally!—so it doesn't even bother him that I like girls."

"So I'll prod around," I grunted.

"Fine. Flavian will give you a once-over-lightly cover of the house and guests. The living is completely informal right now. People do what they want, and eat what they want, whenever they feel so inclined. The dining room runs a kind of open house from breakfast to midnight, so feel free!"

"Thanks," I said. "I—"

There was a sudden shrill squeal from outside, then the door crashed open and a squat-looking guy marched into the room, dragging Eldridge along with him the painful way—with his fingers clamped tight around the protesting Flavian's earlobe.

"I found this little creep with his ear jammed tight

to the keyhole," the guy growled. "Figured you should know about it, Dion."

Freidel sighed deeply. "Flavian was born with a keyhole clamped to one ear, and a pair of binoculars screwed into his eye sockets, Art. I figure he came out of the womb the complete voyeur, so it's too late to change him now."

"Yeah?" The squat guy let go of Eldridge's earlobe with obvious reluctance, then scowled at me. "Who's this?"

"Danny Boyd," Freidel told him. "Danny, meet Art Luman."

Luman was a five-by-five and his vast bulk probably made him look shorter than his actual height. The suit material looked expensive, but on a body shaped like a balloon, it could only drape like sackcloth. He was around forty, I guessed, completely bald except for a small area of soft fuzz on the crown of his head. His face was moonshaped, and the piggy little eyes were almost buried in creases of fat.

"The hotshot private fuzz from New York?" Luman sneered. "At his prices, I wonder the sneer isn't platinum-plated!"

"Luman?" I said politely, like the name was familiar. "Didn't you play the second-lead gorilla in one of those old Tarzan movies?"

The heavy jowls quivered for a couple of seconds. "Save the funnies for Chuck Reilly, my associate," he said softly. "He's got a real strong sense of humor."

"Enough for the both of you?" I asked.

"Dion!" Luman ignored me as he turned toward the fashion designer. "If you're not worried by that little fag having his ear to the keyhole, I guess there's noth-thing I can do. Except hope Boyd proves he's worth all the money he's costing, and soon. If anything happens to foul up the showing of your new collection, you know where it'll leave you, huh?" Without waiting for an answer, he turned around and walked ponderously out of the room.

"What a beastly man!" Eldridge squeaked, once he was sure Luman was safely outside. "He's completely brutalized, Dion; I can't think why you allow him to stay here!"

"You asked for it," Freidel said irritably. "Make yourself useful for a change. Show Danny around the place and introduce him to the other guests."

"Well!" The sullen look persisted on Eldridge's face. "At least you trust me to do that!"

"If you keep bitching at me, I could change my mind," Dion snarled. "I'll see you later, Danny."

"Does everybody else know why I'm here?"

"All the staff do, plus Luman and Harry Kempton." He hesitated for a moment. "I'd just as soon the other guests don't know the real reason."

"So I'm an old buddy from the East, taking a California vacation," I suggested, "and you invited me to stay over for the showing."

"Sounds fine," he nodded. His eyes kind of glazed for a moment. "What was it you figured would keep Stephanie from wriggling around the whole time?"

"A chastity belt," I told him.

"A chastity belt," he repeated in a wondering voice. "You're a genius, Danny!" He closed his eyes, while an expression of ecstasy lit up his face. "Yes, I can see it. Chain metal. Very delicate, nicely subtle. What a magnificently wild idea! And I've just about got the time to do it, too."

"I just hope Stephanie doesn't hold me personally responsible," I said uneasily.

"Stephanie?" He gave me a blank look. "Who in hell was talking about Stephanie?"

"I thought we were." I began to get a nervous feeling at the nape of my neck. "But never mind! Why don't we just forget the whole thing?"

"Forget it?" His eyes widened in horror. "A stroke of genius like that I couldn't forget in a million years!"

"Well"—I looked appealingly at Eldridge—"I guess we have to go see the rest of the place, and meet the rest of the people, and all." Then the glare of pure hatred I was getting from him finally penetrated. "What did I do?" I snarled at him.

"Oh, nothing! Nothing at all!" His shoulders twitched suddenly "I mean, if you're so determined to steal my job right out from under my nose, Mr. Boyd, I guess there's nothing I can do about it." He looked at Freidel for an anguished moment before he burst into tears. "Oh, Dion! How *could* you?"

He ran from the room still sobbing violently and I figured this time, maybe, he was hoping there was a firing squad waiting in the front hall.

"Lenore," Freidel said idly.

"Huh?" I stared at him.

"Lenore Brophy, in the next room down. Tell her who you are, and I said for her to introduce you around."

It sounded simple, like straightforward, even. There was no point in pushing my luck, not after that chastity belt talk and Eldridge's nutty reaction, so I smiled vaguely and backed off toward the door.

"You realize we still have one big problem?" Freidel said suddenly.

"We do?" I muttered, still moving slowly backward.

"Indentations!" He glared at me accusingly. "How would you like having to stand up forever?"

"You're right," I admitted.

"I mean," he raved on as I backed into the hall and carefully closed the door on him, "what kind of a girl is it who'd want a pattern stamped on her fanny every time she sat down?"

I started down the hall toward the next room, my mind whimpering in a deranged kind of way.

Chapter TWO

~~~~~~~~~~

The copper blonde lifted her head and stared at me for a couple of seconds as I came into the room. I stared right back, with no pain at all. She was around twenty-five, with short straight hair that was cut close to her head. Her sapphire-colored eyes were set wide apart above prominent cheekbones, and her mouth was attractively large, with an overhung lower lip. She was wearing a thin black sweater which was pulled tautly over the deep fullness of her breasts, which I immediately saw were unencumbered by a bra. The small nipples prodded the material. Her black wool pants clung tightly to her hips and thighs, and formed an intriguing V at the crotch.

"Lenore Brophy?" I queried.

"That's me." She smiled, showing flawless white teeth. "You look like the answer to a non-virgin's prayer right now, whoever you are."

"Danny Boyd." I only gave her the right profile, because this wasn't the ideal time to drive her clean out of her mind. "Dion said you'd introduce me around to the other guests."

"You're the big detective from New York who's going to solve the cut-up caper for us?" She nodded her own confirmation. "It will be strictly my pleasure to introduce you around. I was about through here, anyway. Who have you met already?"

"Freidel, obviously," I told her, "Eldridge, the house models, and some creep called Luman."

"I'm glad you've met dear Art." She wrinkled her nose in distaste. "That means I don't have to risk getting goosed again today. He looks like an ape, but with all those hands he's got to be an octopus. I guess we should start at the pool—that's where the action is at martini-time."

"Just one thing," I said. "Dion prefers the other guests should think I'm just an old friend visiting for the showing, and not a private detective."

"I'll remember that." She walked across to where I was standing and tucked her arm through mine in an easy gesture. "I'm Lenore—you're Danny—and we're going to get to know each other really well, right?" Suddenly, the yielding fullness of her right breast pressed against my elbow. I was about to respond by increasing the pressure when she withdrew her arm. "I nearly forgot the security bit. Imagine how Dion would flip if I told him it was your fault."

"Forget Dion," I grunted. "Just imagine how *I'd* flip."

"*There's* a thought to intrigue my carnal instincts." She moved away from me, her breasts jiggling freely beneath the black sweater. From the workbench she gathered a mess of embryo dresses in her arms. "Why don't you wait for me out in front of the house while I give these to Dion, so he can lock them away for the night?"

"Fine." I nodded. "I'll give you all of two minutes."

It was closer to ten minutes later when she joined me on the wide stone front stairs. There was a dark brooding look on her face and she didn't say anything at all as we started toward the pool. It didn't worry me. I figured the left profile would bring her back into amorous orbit any time I cared to use it. As we came close to the pool, I saw a couple of females stretched out on individual reclining chairs. Beside them was a real fancy drink-wagon with its own orange-colored umbrella.

"Will you look at the rich bitches?" Lenore Brophy

said under her breath. "I bet they've been here the whole goddamned day!" Then her face smoothed and she smiled brightly as we stopped beside the drink-wagon. "Hi, there!" She flicked her fingers gaily. "I'd like you to meet Dion's friend, Danny Boyd. He's staying over for the showing." She turned toward me. "Danny, this is Polly Peridot—and this is Libby Cathcart."

"Danny Boyd?" The Peridot broad made it sound like some kind of a social disease. "Your father wasn't Douglas Boyd, the steel man, by any chance?"

It was hard to tag her age within five years either way of forty. A rawboned woman, wearing a black bikini over not much flesh at all, her arms and legs muscular and heavy. Her hair was a loose mop of bright curls, dyed to match the color of the drink-wagon's umbrella. Her face was heavily made up, the mouth tight-lipped, and the lazy-lidded eyes were a muddy brown color. One look at her made the whole concept of motherhood ridiculous.

"My father's name was Sean Boyd," I told her. "But he was made of steel. I guess that's why he was worn back down to a small boy by the time he was thirty."

"A humorist!" Her mouth turned down at the corners. "But then, I suppose this ridiculous climate fries everyone's brains in time."

Libby Cathcart, I remembered from Freidel's description, was the New York socialite. There was a worldly look about her that suggested to me that there must have been very little in life she hadn't tried, and that the number of lovers and strange beds must have been legion. She had long black hair that fell gracefully to just below her shoulders; her eyes were dark and slumberous, and her neat oval face had a look of complacency that bordered on arrogance. She was wearing a pink robe that was open just enough for me to see the flanks of her smooth ivory breasts as they swept upward, and a long length of thigh almost all the way up to her hip.

"Are you a Californian, Mr. Boyd?" Her voice was polite and remote, the vowels carefully flattened.

"I'm from Manhattan," I told her. "Wrong side of the park, of course."

"How interesting!" She leaned back in the reclining chair and closed her eyes.

"How about a drink, Danny?" Lenore's voice sounded ghoulishly bright, like the gallant hostess who doesn't give a damn if her husband is locked inside the bedroom with her best girl friend, just as long as the party's a success.

"A martini, thanks," I said.

The small hiatus gave me time to look at the enormous pool built like a figure eight. The twin circles were about fifty feet in diameter, joined together by a narrow connecting channel. I was standing at the edge of the lower pool which looked like it had been designed for frolic—and nonswimmers—because it was no deeper than three feet all over. Away at the top of the other circle was a whole complex of diving boards that ranged in height from three to nine feet. I lit a cigarette, vaguely wondering what kind of a small fortune the mosaic-patterned tiling had cost Freidel, when my mouth sagged open helplessly. A body suddenly appeared in the narrow channel that joined the twin pools and slowly drifted toward me. As it came closer I saw it belonged to a girl who was wearing a sodden evening gown, and floating facedown in the water. I let out a strangled grunt, then spun around to face the three women in back of me.

"Hey!" I yelped. "There's a body in the pool!"

"So what else is new?" the Peridot woman asked in a bored voice.

"This is the first time in a couple of days she's floated down this far," Libby Cathcart said in a mildly-interested soprano. "You think Dion could have reversed the filterflow, or something?"

"Are you both crazy?" I snarled. "There's a dead body in the water and—" I stopped as Lenore gave a sudden snort then exploded with laughter. "—and," I continued feebly, "I figure somebody should do something about it."

"It's not for real, Danny." Lenore thrust the martini into my hand and tried real hard to stop laughing. "I'm sorry, but if you could have seen the look on your face when you turned around! It's only one of those mail-order inflatable rubber dolls that come complete with the impossible forty-twenty-forty vital statistics."

"In an evening gown?" I gibbered.

"That's Dion's idea. The gown is one from his last season's collection. He says the doll floating around in it symbolizes the brief life of high fashion. Last season's creations are all now dead, drowned, and forgotten."

"He's got to be out of his mind," I snarled.

"All fashion designers are showbiz people at heart," Polly Peridot sneered. "The successful ones like Dion, anyway."

"But he's got a magnificent talent, darling," Libby Cathcart murmured, her eyes still closed. "We shouldn't overlook that, should we?"

The older woman's eyes glittered nastily. "So it's you he's sleeping with now? And I thought he'd given me up for tennis, or something equally athletic!" She guffawed loudly. "But then—come to think of it—maybe that's exactly what he has done."

"The way I hear it," the brunette cooed, "nobody will sleep with you anymore, darling. Not unless it's for money, of course."

Polly Peridot got slowly onto her feet, then walked toward the Cathcart girl's chair with a look of grim determination on her gaunt face. Libby stood up to meet her, a vague smile on her lips.

"There are times," Polly said thickly, "when a slap across the face is the only way to deal with a gold-plated bitch!"

"What a coincidence!" Libby's smile broadened. "I was just thinking the same thing."

Her right hand moved swiftly so the open palm slammed across the side of the older woman's face, and made a staccato explosive sound. Right then I expected the whole thing to degenerate into a nasty female brawl but surprisingly enough, the Peridot woman didn't fight back. She just stood there for a long moment, the red imprint of Libby's hand standing out on one cheek like a brand, then suddenly dissolved into tears. Still sobbing loudly, she turned and ran toward the house at an awkward gait. The brunette watched her for a little while, the smile still on her lips, then shrugged her shoulders gracefully.

"Poor Polly," she said in an amused voice. "I think she really is getting old." Then she picked up her towel from the chair and also started toward the house, walked leisurely, humming an off-key tune under her breath. I swallowed my martini in three quick gulps, thrust the empty glass back into Lenore's hands and sank into the reclining chair Libby had just vacated.

"Don't let it faze you, Danny," Lenore grinned at me as she made the fresh drink. "It happens all the time."

"You figure Cathcart is sleeping with Freidel?" I asked with my usual tact.

"Very probably." Lenore gave me the fresh drink, then sat down in the empty chair opposite. "You have to understand that Dion is the greatest bull of all time. If they ran him in the Mexican bullfights, he'd be the undisputed champion, with a magnificent collection of matadors' ears to his credit." She giggled softly. "You don't seriously imagine he needs three permanent house models just to model his designs the whole time?"

"I knew I was in the wrong business the moment I walked into his workroom," I acknowledged. "I wonder he gets the time to design clothes what with three house models, the Cathcart woman"—I stared directly at her face—"and you?"

Her lips tightened for a moment, then she shook her head quickly. "Not me, Danny! Oh, sure, he's made the odd pass, but I'm too good a cutter for him to lose and he knows it. Dion is certainly an attractive man but I'm an old-fashioned girl who doesn't believe in sleeping with her boss."

"I guess all this bull-type activity doesn't go down too well with Eldridge?"

"Are you kidding?" She giggled again. "It drives him halfway out of his mind with frustration. The way Flavian sees it, Dion's interest in women is completely abnormal."

"That's great!" I sighed deeply. "The cut-up caper could be motivated by jealousy, obviously. So who's jealous of Freidel? Wrong question; who isn't jealous of Freidel? The Peridot woman is mad at him because she's out of favor; the three house models are all competing against each other, and Libby Cathcart. She's competing against them, of course, and"—I shook my head dismally—"the hell with it!"

"Don't forget Flavian, who's competing against all of them in particular, and womankind in general," Lenore said sympathetically.

"The one thing I'd like to do right now is forget Eldridge," I grunted. "That special outfit Freidel designed for him is about to give me nightmares, I know it!"

"Talking of nightmares"—she glanced toward the house—"there's one heading this way right this minute."

I followed the direction of her gaze and saw a guy heading toward the pool. As he came closer, I saw he was about my height and maybe twenty pounds heavier, but it looked to be all muscle. His flaming red hair was thick and shaggy, with long sideburns that emphasized the big hooked nose and small narrow-lipped mouth. He was wearing a white knit turtle-necked sport shirt, dark plaid slacks, and rope-soled sandals. The strapwatch on his left wrist was the size of a small wall clock, and made me wonder if he was myopic or just couldn't tell the time too good.

"Chuck Reilly," Lenore said in a hurried whisper. "He fetches and carries for Art Luman. The only difference between them is he's a big muscular creep, while his boss is a fat little creep."

The guy stopped in front of my chair, rested his hands on his hips, and grinned down at me. "You're Boyd?" His voice was a deep baritone and had a kind of inbuilt sneer.

"I'm Boyd," I agreed. "You're Reilly, and this is Santo Bahia, California. You want to take it from there?"

"Mr. Luman wants to talk with you right away." He nodded toward the house. "He's waiting for you."

"I only need a waiter when I'm eating," I told him. "I'll be there after I've finished my drink."

He made a big deal out of checking the small clock on his wrist. "Like Mr. Luman says, time is of the essence, Boyd." His grin widened, showing strong crooked teeth. "So, on your feet!"

"Get lost!" I snarled.

His right hand reached down unhurriedly, gathered a fistful of my lapels, then hauled me straight onto my feet with no apparent effort at all. "Start moving now, Boyd," he growled, "before you get your face dented."

It was a challenge. I took a swig of my martini and smiled apologetically before I threw the rest of it in his face. While he was still spluttering I raised my right leg high in the air—mentally coining a brand-new adage about guys in rope sandals shouldn't play rough—then stomped down hard on the bare toes of his left foot. He let out an agonized shriek, then hopped around in a kind of eccentric war dance. I waited until he got close to the edge of the pool, took a standing jump and butted him hard with my shoulder. He let out another wild whoop the moment before he hit the water, and I backed off fast to avoid the splash.

"You always fight that dirty?" Lenore asked in an interested voice.

"You mean there's another way?" I grunted.

Reilly hauled himself out of the pool and started toward me purposefully, a crazy red glint in his eyes. The way he saw it, I sourly realized, we had only made the pilot film for a television fight series, and he was set on finishing the next thirty-nine episodes. I grabbed a full fifth of gin from the drink-wagon, holding it firmly by the neck, and raised it above my head. Reilly come to a reluctant stop just out of range of the bottle, and glowered at me.

"Come any closer and I'll use it," I said truthfully.

He twitched for a couple of seconds, but he wasn't that stupid. "All right, Boyd," he said thickly, "you'll keep!" Then he trudged back toward the house, dripping water as he went.

"Well!" Lenore sighed heavily after he was out of earshot. "I'm glad that's over. For a moment there, I figured it was going to become one of those to the death things."

I returned the gin to the wagon, and made myself a fresh drink. "The one guy I haven't met is Freidel's partner, Kempton."

"He never gets back here until late in the evening," she said. "I don't think he'd stay here at all except

Dion insists on it. All this kind of crazy living Dion revels in just isn't Harry's style at all."

"So maybe I should go talk with the little fat creep," I wondered. "After I've finished this drink."

"I think maybe you should." Her voice was very casual indeed. "I don't know if Dion happened to mention it, but Luman has a piece of the action."

"He mentioned it. How big a piece?"

"I don't know, but I'd guess it was substantial the way the creep throws his overweight around."

I finished the drink and put the glass down. "You coming with me?"

Lenore shook her head. "I'll stay out here for a while. It's nice and peaceful with nobody around." She smiled softly. "But I'll see you later, Danny, that's for sure."

"You know something?" I studied her carefully for a long moment. "When we first met in your workroom you were genuinely sexy. Now you're just pretending." Then I remembered the long wait out front of the house while she had been returning the embryo dresses to Freidel. "Did something happen between you and Dion?"

"Of course not." She shrugged impatiently.

"Okay." I shrugged back at her. "I guess I can always ask him."

Her teeth bit down sharply into her overhung lower lip. "No, don't do that. Dion is just the kind of bastard who'd tell you." The sapphire eyes had a stormy look in them as she glared at me. "So, all right! I lied to you about never having a relationship with Dion. From the first time I saw those three house models fawning and fighting over him, I swore I'd never get involved. But I guess I didn't figure on just how insidious his charm can be over a period of time. Having surrendered, my vanity insisted I was the only female in his life for the last couple of months, and I was until Libby Cathcart took up residence."

"You had a fight with Freidel over this?" I asked.

She nodded. "I had my suspicions from the time she arrived four days back. Last night I stayed up late with a lousy book, then visited Dion's room at around three. You should have seen them," she said with a small unamused laugh. "There they both were, on the bed, Dion lying back looking as smug as all hell, his hands behind his head while she gave him a blow job. A pretty sight, I must say. And do you know what she had the hide to suggest, the bitch? She said why didn't I come and join them?"

"It could have been interesting," I suggested hopefully.

"That's not my scene. Too many people get in the way. And if it's a warm night ... Anyway, I swore to myself I would never speak to him again except about work, but when I delivered those dresses back to him he had the nerve to tell me nothing had changed between us, that we were grown-up people, and that a little sex here and there ... well, it didn't mean anything. Screwing Libby Cathcart was just good client relations, he said, and we'd be together again after the showing of his new collection when she had gone back to New York."

"That was when you blew your stack?"

She gave me an embarrassed grin. "More than that! I went after him with a pair of cutting shears, but luckily for Dion, he can run faster than me. After about four times around the workbench I was all out of breath and starting to feel kind of stupid. So I tossed the shears onto the bench and walked out of the room."

"Things get better all the time," I said miserably. "You've just given me one more suspect to add to the list."

"Cutting up Dion is more in my line," she snorted. "I wouldn't waste the whole day cutting out his elaborate designs just for the pleasure of hacking them into little pieces at night."

"It makes sense," I admitted, "but then, so do a lot of maniacs until they're proved wrong. Have you been analyzed lately?"

"Not lately." The sparkle came back into her eyes and it looked genuine this time. "If you're real nice to me, Danny, maybe I'll come and lie on your couch tonight. Maybe you can give me an in-depth analysis of my nonfrigidity?"

It was a thought to keep me company on the walk back to the house, right up until the time I found Luman waiting for me in the front hall. His face was a bright pink color and the piggy little eyes obviously yearned to kill me some way that was quick, but still painful. He grabbed hold of my arm and pushed me into a small kind of anteroom off the hall, then slammed the door shut in back of us.

"I've been waiting thirty minutes for you, Boyd," he said in a choked voice, "and that's something I never do for anybody, not even important people!"

"I wouldn't have figured anybody important would ever admit to knowing you, Art," I said generously.

His face turned a deeper shade of pink. "Don't think you can take Chuck that easy again, ever," he snarled. "You were luckier than you'll ever know!"

"Next time I'll sneak up on him and bounce an axhandle off the back of his head," I promised. "If your time's that valuable, why don't you say something instead of just running off at the mouth the whole time?"

He swallowed convulsively. "Maybe you don't know it but I'm a silent partner in Freidel's company. You were his idea, not mine, and I can make him change his mind real fast any time I want. So I'm giving you twenty-four hours from now to find out who's been sabotaging his collection, and stop it. If you don't make it in that time you're out on your ear. Got that, Boyd?"

"Sure," I nodded.

"Then get the hell out of here," he grated. "I've wasted too much time on you already."

Chapter THREE

I left Freidel's car in the hotel carpark, then found my way to the bar on the second floor. There was a tall spare-looking guy waiting by the doorway, the worry in his eyes magnified by the thick lens of his black-framed glasses. He smiled uncertainly and took a step toward me as I got close. "Mr. Boyd?"

"If you're Harry Kempton, maybe we should have a password," I said. "What's with all this cloak-and-dagger bit?"

"I'll explain inside." He brushed his hand quickly through the thinning gray hair on top of his head. "It's all very complicated, and I'm sure we can both use a drink."

The Luau Bar I remembered from previous visits to Santo Bahia. It specialized in meager rum-based drinks served in an imitation coconut half-shell at twice the price of good honest liquor. I settled for a martini with a twist of lemon, and Kempton did the same. After the drinks had been served he looked around nervously, then whispered, "I think we can talk safely now, Mr. Boyd."

"Freidel dragged me into a corner and told me to meet you here," I said curiously. "Then gave me his car keys and said I should try not to be seen leaving the house. What the hell are you, exactly? Some kind of a reject CIA agent?"

He picked up his martini and examined it carefully, like it could be some esoteric type of hemlock, before he took a cautious sip. "We intended to keep you a secret—your profession that is, Mr. Boyd—just between the two of us. Then Dion told Eldridge and, I guess, Eldridge told Art Luman. So then the secret didn't matter anymore and Dion told the rest of his staff about you. Have you had any conversation with Luman?"

"Twenty-four hours to solve the cut-up caper, or I get tossed out on my ear," I said. "What makes Luman the villain around here? I understood he's a silent partner in your company?"

"That's precisely the trouble, Mr. Boyd." Kempton removed his glasses and blinked at me myopically. "In the beginning, Dion was a brilliant fashion designer with no conception of either manufacturing or distribution, so he came to me. I had the know-how to launch him into the medium-high-priced market, but I didn't have the capital it would take. The regular sources of finance were closed to us because they wouldn't risk their money on a then-unknown designer. Finally I went to Art Luman and he put up the money under certain specific conditions."

"Like what?" I queried.

"Specifically, that if the company loses money in any one financial year, he has the right to buy out the both of us at the par value of our stockholding. This would be about one fifth of its true value, of course. Although our turnover has been up this year, the expenses have more than matched it so far. That crazy chateau setup of Dion's costs a fortune in upkeep! In fact, unless the new spring collection has a great success, we are going to wind up the financial year in the red."

"You figure that's just what Luman wants to happen?"

"Yes." He replaced his glasses back onto his nose in a decisive gesture. "When Dion invited a couple of his major clients—who were both good for a lot of publicity about the showing—to stay over at the house, Luman insisted both he and Reilly should also be invited. Then Dion insisted I should be a houseguest, to keep an eye on Luman." He shook his head sorrowfully. "I'm just no good at that kind of thing, Mr. Boyd. So when all the trouble started, I suggested to Dion we should get a professional to deal with it."

"How come you chose me?"

"I have a friend on the local police force who recommended you." His smile was strictly nervous. "Well, to be honest, he said a lot of very rude things about you, but then admitted you did get results. You may remember him—Lieutenant Schell?—he remembers you very distinctly."

I got a sudden twinge deep in my stomach. During both my previous visits to Santo Bahia, I'd tangled with Schell and wound up in a kind of Mexican standoff. For some crazy reason of his own, he was convinced that wherever I went, a mound of corpses piled up rapidly in back of me.

"I remember the lieutenant, also very distinctly," I said. "You figure it could be Luman in back of the sabotage?"

"I don't want to think that about him," he said glumly. "But he's the only one with a logical motive, wouldn't you agree?"

"Maybe logic has nothing to do with it." I shrugged. "With your partner running his female staff like they're working in his private harem, there has to be a whole stack of jealousy running loose, too."

"I know!" He looked like he was going to bust out crying. "I've spoken severely to Dion about it many times, but he claims he's an artist and needs romance the whole time to inspire him."

"Not to mention sex," I added. "What do you know about Art Luman's background?"

"Not very much," Kempton said cautiously. "He's a fringe operator, of course, and works out of Los Angeles. I've tried to check his background but nobody seems to know anything about him down there. Either that, or they just won't give the information. To be honest, Mr. Boyd, he makes me feel nervous everytime I'm in the same room with him. There's a whole aura of violence about the man. Have you met his so-called associate, Reilly?"

"Sure," I nodded.

"I can't help feeling he's just Luman's strong-arm man, and if Luman intends to ensure the company shows a loss this financial year, he won't stop at sabotaging the collection. If that doesn't work for him, I'm sure he'll go to any lengths to achieve his purpose!"

"This is all supposition," I said. "You don't have any proof."

"I know," he nodded quickly. "I just wanted to put the true facts of Luman's interest in the company before you, Mr. Boyd, so you can be on your guard."

"You've done that just fine," I told him. "How about another drink?"

"If you don't mind, Mr. Boyd"—he got that agent-on-the-run look back on his face—"I think I'll leave now, and drive straight out to Dion's place. It will be safer if we don't both arrive back there too close together."

"How long has Luman had you bugged like this?" I asked.

"Ever since I've had to live under the same roof with him, I suppose." He made a painful effort at a grin. "It sounds stupid even to me, but I'm afraid I just can't help it."

"He doesn't affect Freidel the same way?"

"Nothing ever affects Dion, Mr. Boyd! He's completely wrapped inside his own ego. The only reason other people exist is to carry out his orders." He jumped up quickly onto his feet. "I must go now. Please remember our little meeting never even happened so far as anyone else, except Dion, is concerned."

"Okay." I shrugged resignedly. "If you happen to meet a dwarf wearing a trench coat and dark glasses on your way out, don't forget to duck!"

The look on his face as he walked away from the table said he didn't think that was funny at all. Maybe he was right. For sure, I figured sourly, the two of them made a great partnership. Kempton was scared limp that Luman was laying for the company, while Freidel was so busy laying all those females in his private harem, he didn't have the time to be scared about anything. Meanwhile—back at the chateau—the chances were that cut-up was probably busy flexing his, or her, shears, ready for another night's sabotage.

I ate a quick steak in the hotel restaurant, then picked up Freidel's car and drove back to his private nuthouse. The guard checked me out carefully before he let me through the gates, and by the time I parked in front of the house the butler already had the front door open.

"Good evening, sir." He greeted me as I stepped into the front hall in a voice that somehow reminded me of an overripe Stilton cheese. "Mr. Freidel requests the pleasure of your company in the bar."

"It sounds like a good place to get pleasured," I allowed. "Where do I find it?"

"The second floor, sir. Turn right at the head of the stairs, and it's the third room to your left."

I followed his instructions and wound up in a large room that had a marble-topped bar running the full length of one wall. Freidel was installed behind it, playing bartender, while a couple of the house models were perched on barstools sipping something out of tall glasses. Deborah, the cool redhead, was wearing a brown shift, while Kitty, the blonde, had on what looked like a man's shirt that fitted her delightfully plump torso so tight it might have been sprayed on her. They both turned their heads and watched with welcoming smiles as I headed toward the bar.

"It's not Robert Redford," Kitty declared throatily.

"Who needs Robert Redford?" Deborah said with a shake of her head. "We have to make do with what we've got in hand, so to speak."

"Anyway, I saw him first." Kitty's ripe breasts strained against the shirt. The hem of it had ridden right up her thigh, and I glimpsed a brief flash of white at the top of her thigh where it thickened out to the curve of her buttocks.

"We don't have to *fight* about it, darling," the redhead purred. "There's more than enough there for both of us." Her eyes dropped meaningfully to my groin where a tiny flicker of response was sparked. "Maybe there are a few things we can show him."

"Beat it, you two!" Freidel growled.

Kitty pouted at him. "What's the matter with you? Don't you want us to have any fun at all?"

"After the showing," he said. "Before then, it's work, work, work!"

Kitty made a whole production out of sliding off the barstool. As her legs slid down toward the floor, the hem of her shirt stayed right where it was. Her briefs were small and semi-transparent. A creamy swell of hair pressed against them, strands of it escaping from beneath them along the insides of her thighs. She gave me a slow, sleepy smile, and pulled the shirt down again.

"Bitch!" the redhead said under her breath. "A born exhibitionist. Still, when you've got glandular trouble..."

"Don't be bitter," Kitty said sweetly. "It makes your face all crinkle up, and when that happens, it shows your age."

I watched them until they left the room, my eyes

glazing with the effort of trying to decide which one I preferred, then deciding that the three of us could have a mighty nice time together. I thought I would work on it.

"Maybe you need a drink." There was a touch of acid in Freidel's voice.

"Rye, on the rocks." I climbed onto the nearest barstool. "You worried I might pick up a piece of the action in your private harem?"

He finished making the drink and pushed the glass toward me across the marble bartop. "Just resolve my sabotage problem, Danny, and I'll make you an honorary sultan afterward!" He went carefully through his moustache-brushing ritual. "How did you make out with Harry Kempton?"

"You sure have a tiger for a partner there," I said.

"Poor old Harry!" He chuckled. "It scares the pants off him everytime Art Luman sneezes."

"But Luman doesn't faze you any?"

"Nobody and nothing fazes me," he said with conviction. "I guess Harry told you all about the company setup?"

"Which gives Luman a strong motivation to ruin your new collection." I nodded. "I can understand Luman wanting to buy out Kempton's stock at a big profit, but if he buys you out he doesn't have the big-name designer anymore."

"The Freidel label would still have value," he said, "even without me."

"I guess that figures," I agreed. "The other motive is jealousy, and you've given just about every woman around here good reason."

"I have?" He made a lousy try at looking modest.

"The three house models were all tossed aside for Lenore Brophy, who in turn was tossed aside for Libby Cathcart," I said in a kind of recital. "Polly Peridot doesn't take kindly to the idea of Libby gracing your bed, either. And, of course, all this wild heterosexual activity on your part is driving Eldridge beserk."

"You have been a busy little ferret, haven't you?" He took his time about lighting a long thin panatela cigar. "It sounds like you've got plenty there to keep you busy, Danny."

"Plenty of motivation but no proof," I said, "and not much time, either. Luman gave me twenty-four hours to come up with an answer, or get tossed out on my ear."

"There's Art for you." He grinned wryly. "Impulsive!"

"You go along with him?"

"I don't have any choice, Danny." He spread his hands wide, unconsciously giving a brilliant imitation of a Lebanese horsetrader. "I know it's unfair to you—stupid, even!—but right now I can't afford to cross Luman."

I heard the quick padding of bare feet on the floor and turned my head to see Stephanie, the tall dark house model, coming toward the bar with a set look of fury on her face. She was wearing a canary-yellow ankle-length dress, the neckline of which showed a generous display of cleavage. Her full breasts moved independently of the rest of her. Beneath the dress I could just make out their free-swinging contours.

"Dion," she hissed, "if you don't stop that little maniac from hounding me around the house, I'll—"

"*Dion!*" It was a cry from the heart as Eldridge ran into the room with tears in his eyes. "Make her take it off!"

"Sounds like a great idea," I said enthusiastically.

"Children!" Freidel glared at the both of them. "Just what the hell is this all about?"

"That marvelous dress she's wearing," Eldridge babbled. "It's one from the new collection and it should be locked away with the others for the night." He came to a skidding halt in front of the model and snarled at her. "If you don't take it off right now"—his off-key treble wavered for a moment, then hardened with determination—"I will!"

"Drop dead!" she sneered.

He lunged forward, and reaching right down, grabbed the hem of the dress with both hands and managed to pull it up to her knees before Stephanie reacted. She bunched her slender fingers into a small fist and hit him straight between the eyes. He let out a heartrending shriek as he reeled backward away from the bar until he cannoned into the side of an armchair. I watched admiringly as he performed an involuntary somersault right across the seat of the chair and hit the floor on the far side with a resounding crash.

Freidel sighed softly. "The dress?" he inquired.

"It was Lenore's idea," Stephanie said, as if nothing important had happened. The yellow material dipped in between the rise of her breasts. "She was worried about the cut. You know how you're always telling us to model any of your creations the way we feel about it when we're wearing it." Her fingers plucked impatiently at the dress. "I'll be modeling this at the showing, and Lenore wanted to be sure it felt right, so she asked me to wear it for a while. Don't worry about anything happening to it tonight." She laughed shortly. "I'll either wear it to bed, or sleep with it under the pillow, or something."

There was a faint bleating sound from Eldridge as he managed to totter onto his feet, then collapse into the armchair. "I'm sure," he said in a muffled voice, "there's something broken!"

"Your wooden head, I hope," Freidel snapped. "I guess that's okay, Stephanie, but don't let the dress out of your sight."

"I won't," she promised. "Thanks, Dion."

She stopped for a moment beside the armchair on

her way out of the room and gave Eldridge a consoling pat on top of his head. "Never mind, Flavian," she purred. "I'm sure nothing vital was broken or you'd be speaking in a baritone now, wouldn't you?" Then she continued blithely on her way, ignoring his thin screech of outraged fury.

"Where is this room you keep everything locked up for the night?" I asked.

"The next floor up." Freidel made himself another drink. "Why?"

"I'd like to see it," I told him.

"Okay. Let's finish this drink first." He looked across at the inert figure in the armchair. "You want a drink, Flavian?"

"I'm dying!" Eldridge waved a limp hand in the air. "Dying!"

"I'm not sure if death benefits are included in your contract." The designer thought about it for a few seconds, then a dreamy look came into his eyes. "But, if you don't mind being stuffed, I'll personally pick up the taxidermist's tab. Then I could have you mounted on a pedestal in the front hall, swathed from head to foot in floating white tulle, holding a wand in your right hand to represent the fashion magic woven by Dion Freidel. How does that grab you?"

Eldridge pulled himself out of the armchair and limped slowly across the room until he reached the doorway, then gave Freidel a stricken look. "Dion," he said in a trembling voice, "you are a monster!"

Freidel grinned at me after the door closed. "The room?"

"The room," I agreed, and finished my drink.

Some thirty seconds later he unlocked the door of the storage room on the top floor and we went inside. The walk-in closet was stacked with finished garments ready for the showing, and there was a large desk littered with unfinished bits and pieces. An ancient couch completed the furnishings. I walked over to the window and looked down, seeing how the underwater lighting displayed the twin circular pools to advantage at night.

"The wall is sheer from the ground up," Freidel said. "It would need a human fly to get in the window."

"Maybe," I said. "Who lives directly across the hall?"

"I do. Libby Cathcart has the guestroom next to mine, and Polly Peridot is next door on this side."

I put the flat of my hand on the seat of the couch and pressed hopefully. It didn't give an inch. "What do I have to lose but my spine?" I said morosely. "I'll stay here the night."

"You think that's necessary?" He winced when he saw the look on my face.

"Okay, it was a stupid question."

"I'll take a shower first, then slip into something loose for the rest of the night," I said.

"Sure, I'll take you to your room." Freidel locked the door in back of us, then I followed him down the hallway to a room on the other side of the house.

"Sims put you in good company." A satyr's leer showed up underneath his moustache. "You've got Deborah on one side of you, Kitty on the other, and Stephanie right across the hall."

"If it gets too dull in the storeroom, maybe I can get a game of strip poker going." I suggested.

He handed me the key to the storeroom. "I leave the safety of the Freidel collection in your hands for the night, Danny. If you feel like joining me for an early morning swim around seven, I'll see you at the pool."

After he had gone I had a shower and got dressed in a sport shirt, slacks, and a pair of rubber-soled shoes. Then I collected a few necessities for the night like cigarettes, the bottle of rye I carried around for like emergencies when other people's booze wasn't available, a glass from the bathroom and—the one thing I hoped I wouldn't need—the thirty-eight from the bottom of my bag, still holstered in the shoulder rig. I emptied the rest of my clothes and junk from the bag, put the necessities into it and went back to the storeroom. Once inside I locked the door behind me, unpacked the bag and made myself a drink. Maybe a half hour and a couple of drinks later, I felt tired. It had been a long, hard and singularly unrewarding day, so I stretched out on the cast-iron couch and closed my eyes.

When I opened my eyes again, sunlight was streaming into the room. My watch said it was ten after six, and my back felt like it was broken in five separate places. I groaned as I sat up, the taste in my mouth unspeakable, and Freidel's suggestion about an early morning swim suddenly sounded like a brilliant idea. So I repacked my bag, locked the storeroom, and went back to my own room. After cleaning my teeth and shaving the profile, I changed into a pair of tartan trunks which the guy in Brooks Brothers had assured me even Scotsmen were wearing this year. I carefully zipped the storeroom key into the hip pocket, grabbed a towel, and headed toward the life healthy.

The Californian morning was warming up with the sun shining brightly out of a cloudless blue sky. By the time I reached the lower pool, even my back had stopped creaking. I stuck one big toe fearlessly into the water and it didn't turn blue, or anything. Then some kind of an instant insanity hit me, and I decided to go into the pool in style. As I headed toward the upper pool that goddamned inflatable rubber doll—still wearing its sodden evening gown—came floating through the narrow joining channel and momentarily had me gibbering.

When I reached the complex of diving boards, I

carefully climbed onto the lowest one, then took a deep breath. In a moment, I thought smugly, I was about to bounce off the springy end, describe a beautiful arc through the air, then cut into the water clean as a knife blade. Everything went just fine right up until the moment my foot slipped just as I was leaving the springy end. So instead of describing that beautiful arc, I lunged forward into the air with my arms flailing wildly and hit the water horizontally. The impact took the breath out of my lungs, and my stomach felt like it had been slit wide open by a serrated knife. I also made the mistake of opening my mouth to scream a little, and swallowed a mouthful of chlorinated water for my trouble. By the time I surfaced I had just one thought; to reach the edge of the pool the quickest way I knew how, then forget all about the healthy life for the rest of my stay in Santo Bahia. Three frantic strokes brought me to the edge of the pool and I hauled myself out real fast, grabbed the towel and started to dry myself. Then, once the water was out of my eyes, I saw that inflatable doll drifting slowly toward me.

It didn't make any sense. Hardly a minute back I had seen it float into the lower pool, and now it was back again. I rubbed my eyes with the towel some more, took a second look, and got that hollow feeling in my legs. If that was the same inflatable rubber doll, my mind shrieked at me, how come it had changed into a canary-yellow dress? I dived back into the water, swam a few yards until I was close enough to grab the nearest arm, then towed the body back to the side. Then I scrambled out onto the edge of the pool, knelt down and lifted the body out. The solid weight told me—as the feel of the cold flesh already had—that this was no imitation woman.

I lay the body on its back beside the pool, and the wide-open eyes of the brunette house model stared up at me in unblinking horror. Her mouth still framed a silent scream, and she was wearing a dark red necklace around her throat where it had been slit, almost from ear to ear.

Chapter FOUR

The hooded gray eyes under the close-cropped gray hair stared at me with open distaste. "I left you until last, Boyd," Lieutenant Schell said, "I guess it's the masochist in me."

"It gave me time to eat breakfast," I said, "then sit around twiddling my thumbs and growing old for the next three hours."

"I was out of my mind to recommend you to Harry Kempton," he rasped. "Bug-eyed Boyd—the East Coast corpse-magnet!—where he goes, murder victims start to fall out of the woodwork. This used to be a quiet town, you know that? A few loaded tourists, a few bum checks, a couple of domestic brawls was all. Now, everytime you turn up in Santo Bahia, the way the bodies follow you around it's like murder was going out of style."

"It was only coincidence I found the body," I protested.

"With you, there is no such thing as coincidence," he snarled. "How did you know she was there?"

"I didn't," I said. "I just happened to be the first one to go for a swim this morning."

"After supposedly spending the night in the storeroom," he sneered. "Freidel told me about that; you locked yourself in with the key, so you could get out anytime you wanted."

"I spent the night there," I grated. "Why the hell would I want to kill Stephanie, anyway? I only met the girl yesterday afternoon!"

"Maybe somebody hired you."

"You know Kempton hired me"—I bared my teeth at him—"on your recommendation."

"So somebody could have made a you a better offer last night?"

I began to get that uneasy feeling I always got after I had been talking to Schell for a while, something like a woodpecker remorselessly drilling its beak into my skull. "It's the reverse psychology bit," I said slowly. "You don't believe any of this crap you're feeding me, but you hope I'll be convinced you do believe it, so I'll run faster to try and solve your murder for you because you'll have me running scared."

He leaned back in his chair and rolled his eyes at the ceiling. "Now I've heard everything! If you want my honest opinion of you, Boyd, you'd offer your own mother protection for a hundred bucks a day and if somebody offered you the same—plus fringe benefits—to kill her, you'd deliver her body before the week was out."

"The last time you were honest was when you were in knee-pants," I told him. "Your mother didn't take you seriously and it created an embarrassing situation in the local supermart!"

"I didn't get you in here to trade insults," he said in a kind of regretful voice. "I know why Kempton hired you, so what have you found out?"

"Not much," I admitted. "All of it you probably know by now. Luman has got a good motive to want Freidel's new collection to fail, so he can buy both him and Kempton out cheap. Freidel himself is a kind of super stud, so just about every woman in the house is jealous of him with good reason."

He nodded impatiently. "Sure, I know that. So what else is new?"

I shrugged. "You tell me."

"The last person to see the girl alive was that blond model, Kitty. She says Stephanie came into her room just before midnight and talked for a while, mainly bitching about how impossible Eldridge had been over the dress she was wearing. There was an earlier argument about that, and she clobbered him. You saw it, right?" I nodded, and he continued. "She left Kitty's room around a half hour later and said she was going to bed. The coroner figures the time of death someplace between two and three A.M. At that time everyone in the house was asleep, they claim! The murderer has to be living inside this crazy mansion because I checked out the guards on night duty at the gates. It so happens they're both ex-cops known to me, and when they say nobody came in or out during the whole night, I'll believe them."

"Where was she killed?" I asked.

"That's a good question."

"You're kidding!"

"Her throat was cut," he said bleakly. "There should have been a lot of bloodstains someplace. We've been through the house—and the grounds—with that proverbial fine-tooth comb, and haven't found a trace."

I thought for a moment. "The pool?"

"Your eyes weren't seeing so good this morning," he sneered. "There was still some blood hanging around in patches in the shallow pool, and a couple of smears on the tiled edge in one place. Cut a throat and you sever a main artery, then get so much blood that even dilution, chlorine and filtration can't make it disappear entirely. It makes for a weird picture; the murderer entices her out of the house in the middle of the night. When they reach the edge of the pool he jumps in with her to cut her throat."

"It had to be somebody she knew and trusted," I said. "But then she knew everybody who was inside the house last night."

"Sure she knew the killer," he barked, "but she didn't necessarily have to trust him. He could have held the knife at her throat and forced her to go out of the house with him. We haven't found the murder weapon yet, incidentally."

"Motive?" I queried.

He shook his head. "Not unless you figure Eldridge was capable of killing her just because she wouldn't take off that dress. The way he looks, he couldn't kill a fly—just doesn't have the strength for it!"

"The dress was part of the new collection," I said tentatively, "and now it's ruined. Maybe there's a link between that and whoever's been sabotaging the collection before?"

"Half a thread is better than none at all?" Schell raised his eyebrows sardonically. "The whole trouble here is you aren't dealing with normal people. The whole goddamned bunch of them are crazy, and I do include you."

"So what are you going to do now, Lieutenant?" I asked smugly.

"Wait for the autopsy report—see what L.A. can dig up on Luman for me—then come back later and ask the same questions all over again." His hooded eyes looked at me challengingly. "What the hell else can I do?"

"You're right," I agreed.

"I've told them, especially the Peridot and Cathcart women, that everyone has the freedom of Santo Bahia but nobody leaves town. That includes you, of course." He yawned elaborately. "Oh, there is one more thing. I figure it would be a big help to have somebody planted on the inside. A very special kind of guy with no scruples at all; a polished liar, with the morals of a tomcat."

"You mean you've got a cop like that working for you?" I asked incredulously.

"Not yet, but I'm swearing him in as a special deputy." His grin reminded me of a gray nurse shark I saw one time in northern Australia. "You!"

"Me?" My voice jumped an octave. "You're out of your mind!"

"You hold a New York State private detective's license," he said in a tranquil voice, "which means you're not licenced to operate in this state. But I've decided—since you generously offered to cooperate by volunteering to become a special deputy—to ignore the legality of your position. I expect you to report immediately when you discover anything of consequence regarding this homicide and I do mean both immediately, and anything."

"What do I do?" I almost choked on the words. "Hold up my right hand and swear to be a good little Boyd and do like the lieutenant says the whole time?"

"I don't think we need go through the formalities," he murmured. "When I get back downtown, I'll just make a note that D. Boyd was today sworn in as a special deputy. If you want to deny it later that's okay, nobody will believe you."

"Yes, sir, Lieutenant," I muttered. "Is there anything more, Lieutenant, sir?"

"Just keep one thing in mind," he said coldly. "The private guards will keep out the reporters, but this homicide is going to be big news all over the country. I'm not about to be tagged as some hick local cop who can't handle it, so if anyone's going to be tossed to the wolves, I'm starting with you."

"Okay," I snarled. "Be smart and make it a two-way deal, like tell me if you come up with anything interesting, huh?"

"Why not?" The shark-toothed grin came back onto his face. "Well, Deputy, I guess that's about all for now."

I walked out of the anteroom into the front hall, silently checking out Schell's ancestry in a vivid pattern of four-letter words. Maybe fresh air would help me cool off, I figured, so I went out of the house and walked aimlessly toward the pool. As I got closer I saw the gaunt figure of Polly Peridot standing on the edge, staring blankly at the water. She turned her head as she heard my footsteps coming close, and I saw her skin had a gray drawn look underneath the heavy makeup. Her heavy-lidded eyes were even muddier than usual, while the mop of bright orange curls on top of her head gave her a curiously surrealistic, kind of grotesque Harpo Marx image.

"I can't stop thinking about that poor girl," she said in a low voice. "Floating around all alone in the darkness with her throat—" She swallowed convulsively. "What time is it, Mr. Boyd?"

I checked my watch. "A quarter of twelve."

"I need a drink." She smiled wanly. "Make me a martini, please?"

"Sure, Polly," I said.

"Thank you, Danny." There was a slight sneer in her voice. "Murder is a great leveler, isn't it?"

The drink-wagon was waiting beside the pool, restocked with clean glasses and shining with a kind of aseptic glitter. In Freidel's establishment it figured that murder was a sometime thing, but drinking went on forever. I made a couple of Boydsized martinis and handed her one. She took two gulps which about halved the contents of the Old-Fashioned glass, then sat down on one of the reclining chairs.

"This helps," she acknowledged. "Poor Stephanie! According to that terrifying police lieutenant—the one with absolutely no manners at all!—it had to be one of the people staying in the house last night who killed her. I just can't believe any one of us would be capable of such a dreadful thing."

"One of us is either a homicidal maniac or had good reason for killing her," I said flatly.

She shivered. "I don't want to even think about it anymore. At least Dion had enough taste left to remove that idiotic inflatable doll from the pool after what happened last night."

"I figure he's got taste in about everything, especially women," I said casually. "Libby Cathcart is a real dish."

Her mouth tightened. "He's a great stud, if that's what you mean. Dion is singularly adept at using any woman he thinks can help further his career. I've never met a man like him before who's so completely devoid of all natural feelings, like loyalty and gratitude. If it hadn't been for me he never would have got his start, but he's forgotten that already." Her laugh was a harsh unpleasant sound. "It was me who made it possible for him to quit that nothing job in a department store and concentrate on designing until he came up with enough original ideas to interest somebody like Harry Kempton in a partnership. So now he's got it made, I don't interest him anymore."

"Maybe he figures Libby Cathcart can do more for him now?" I suggested.

"And she's twenty years younger than I am," Polly Peridot said dryly. "There was a time when I could get away with it, in spite of being a freak! I could give them their jollies in all kinds of interesting ways the unimaginative males hadn't thought of before, but now all that lovely juvenile vitality has gone." Her mouth twisted as she looked down at herself. "I'm just an old mare—and I look it!—and they should have taken me to the glue factory years back. But he's making a bad mistake with that little Cathcart bitch."

"Why is that?" I asked interestedly.

"She's one of the black widow variety. The last thing she wants is for Dion to be a success, because that makes him unobtainable on a permanent basis. What she wants is for him to have a resounding failure that will give her a chance to pick up the pieces. Libby would like nothing better than make him Mr. Cathcart, so she can show him off to all her society friends. Her new husband, the fashion designer, who now only designs for just one person—her!"

"How far would she push it?"

The muddy brown eyes gave me an appraising, suddenly shrewd, look. "To the point of committing murder, you mean? I don't know. Much as I hate the little bitch, I don't honestly think she'd go that far. Who knows? I've been wrong about people most of my life, so maybe she's no exception." She held out her empty glass to me. "You make a mean martini the first time around. See if you can do it again."

I made the fresh drink and gave it to her. She drank about two thirds of the contents like it was milk, then came up for air. "It's a day for getting loaded," she said in a dull voice. "It's also no big secret around here that you're the private detective they hired to stop someone making a massacre out of Dion's new collection. Now that's something I wouldn't put past Libby!"

"I had you figured as a tooth-and-claw girl," I said. "After Libby Cathcart slapped you last night, I was real surprised when you just turned on the waterworks and ran."

"It was one of my lesser days." She grimaced sharply. "I seem to be getting a hell of a lot of those lately. I guess what hurt was the truth. The little bitch was right when she said nobody leaps into my bed anymore unless they've been paid for it first." She tilted her head upward and looked at me with a mocking glint in her eyes. "You look like you could be the same class of stud as Dion. How about it, Danny? What's your going price for spending a night with your Aunt Polly?" The negligent wave of her hand said I didn't need bother about answering. "The trouble is I'm running out of money fast. That last nogoodnik I married took me to the cleaners over the divorce."

"You want me to bust out crying?"

"You're an arrogant son-of-a-bitch, Danny Boyd." She chuckled throatily. "I used to like myself better when I was that way, too. Why don't you get the hell out of here while I feed my memories of used-to-was with a few more martinis?"

I put my empty glass on the drink-wagon and started back toward the house. The front door was wide open, so I walked through the front hall, knocked on the door of Freidel's workroom and opened it. He was sitting on the end of the workbench, his shoulders hunched, puffing a cloud of blue smoke from his thin cigar.

"You look creative," I said as I walked farther into the room. "Or else that look on your face is one hell of a good excuse for doing nothing."

"I was thinking about Stephanie," he said softly. "She was a good kid. Why in hell would anybody want to kill her?"

"It's a good question," I said.

"She wasn't like the other two, Kitty and Deborah," he continued in the same reflective voice. "Stephanie wasn't the brightest girl in the world but she could model a certain kind of fashion like nobody else could in the whole business." His voice grew wistful for a moment. "In bed, she was a one-girl cyclone!"

"Everybody has sex on their minds this morning," I growled. "Polly Peridot is worried because she has to pay cash on the barrelhead for a horizontal companion these days, and she's runnning out of cash fast. She's also worried about Libby Cathcart hoping you'll go broke so she can put a marital collar around your neck, then show you off to her friends as the tame husband who now only designs for one person in the whole world—her."

"That Polly," he said coldly, "she has a big mouth."

"Maybe she's a truth-sayer?"

"If you're thinking it could have been Libby who killed Stephanie, forget it," he snapped. "Libby was with me last night until about five thirty this morning."

"Did the lieutenant buy that?" I sneered.

"I didn't bother trying to sell it to him," Freidel said. "But I know two people who couldn't have murdered Stephanie. You please yourself about believing it, Danny."

"I'll take a raincheck," I told him. "What's going to happen about showing the new collection now?"

"We go right ahead with it." He gave me a vaguely surprised look. "It's too bad about Stephanie, but the whole world can't just fall apart because she was murdered!"

"You're all heart, Dion," I said, and left him perched on the edge of the workbench contemplating, I guessed, the very finite world of Dion Freidel.

The next door down the front hall took me into Lenore Brophy's workroom. She was wearing a knit dress that clung possessively to her rich curves, drawn tight over her breasts and button-like nipples, tracing the rise of her stomach and flattened over her thighs.

"It seems like a couple of months since I last saw you, Danny." She pouted that overhung lip at me. "I thought we had a date last night," she said reproachfully. "There I was, all willing and ready. I snuck into your room, but you weren't there. So where were you? It was either Kitty, or Deborah, that's for sure. Or both."

"I was in the storeroom," I groaned. "Breaking my back on that cast-iron couch, fearlessly protecting the collection while somebody was busy murdering Stephanie."

She shivered slightly. "It gives me the creeps to even think about the poor kid! Who could have—"

"Don't ask," I interrupted her. "I've heard the question too many times already, but nobody's come up with the answer yet. What time was it when you went into my room?"

"About a quarter of one this morning. My room is on the opposite side of the hallway to yours, right at the end. Kitty is straight across from me and I heard her and Stephanie talking for a while until Stephanie came back into her own room, next door to mine. I wanted to be sure they'd both settled down for the night before I went into your room." She grinned ruefully. "Boy! Was I ever wasting my time!"

"You didn't see anybody else in the hallway?"

"No." She hesitated for a long moment. "I didn't tell the lieutenant this, because I figured it was none of his business and it wouldn't help him anyway. But I got so mad when I found you weren't in your room, figuring you'd shacked up with one of the house models for the night, I decided to find out what kind of a welcome I'd get from Dion. I tippytoed all the way down to his room and knocked discreetly on the door. Guess what? The miserable bastard called out, 'Come right on in, *Libby*.' For a moment there I debated if I should cut his heart out, but then I got a better idea. The door to the Cathcart woman's room wasn't locked so I went straight in without knocking. She was preening herself in front of the dresser mirror, wearing a whole elaborate see-through negligee, obviously about to visit her beloved next door. I told her I'd just stopped by to spare her any possible embarrassment, on my way to spend the night in Dion's room. You should have seen her face! She almost spat straight in my eye. By the time I got back to my own room again, I figured the whole thing had been almost worth it."

"You figure it kept her out of Freidel's room for the whole night?" I asked casually.

"I'll give you any odds you like it did," Lenore said

in a confident voice. "Any girl in her situation would lock her door, go to bed, and if Dion came asking later, tell him his precise fortune. No fury like, and etcetera, especially if the woman concerned is told by another woman that she's being scorned!"

She picked up a piece of black velvet from the top of her workbench. "But neither death nor sexual intrigue must stop the Freidel collection from being ready on time. Dion made that explicitly clear to me just a few minutes back. What the hell did I do with my shears?" She searched around in the heap of cuttings on the bench top unsuccessfully, then pulled open the top drawer irritably. "I never, I know, put them away in here, so why am I looking—" The color suddenly drained out of her face. "Danny!"

"Libby Cathcart's hiding in there with Freidel?" I asked brightly.

"Danny, please!" Her voice shook. "Look at this."

I moved up beside her and looked down at the open drawer. The cutting shears were there all right, the blades stained a dull red color.

"Lieutenant Schell will give you a big 'E' for effort," I said in a neutral voice. "He had the whole house searched this morning and couldn't find the murder weapon."

"Oh, my God!" Lenore whispered. "You mean somebody used my shears to kill Stephanie?"

"You want to think up some good answers for the lieutenant, honey," I said. "They're your shears and you used them to chase Freidel around your workbench only the other evening, as I remember."

"Then I threw them onto the workbench and walked out to meet you." Her eyes were large and round as she stared at me. "That was the last time I saw them, up until a moment back, I swear!"

"You don't have to convince me," I said truthfully, "just the lieutenant."

Chapter FIVE

Like Freidel had told me, the dining room ran a continuous buffet service all through the day up to around ten in the evening. So it was no problem to get some lunch at three in the afternoon. Schell had been and gone, taking the murder weapon with him. He had questioned Lenore for some forty minutes before letting her go and she had retired, red-eyed, to her room. I hadn't been expecting the special deputy's medal of honor or anything like that, just a few words of humble thanks from the lieutenant would have been enough. All I got from Schell was a filthy look on his way out, and a growled negative when I asked if he'd made any progress.

Luman and Reilly came into the dining room just as I was finishing my lunch, and I was grateful they had left it until then so the sight of them both hadn't put me off my food. Fatso was wearing another expensive-looking and shapeless suit, while Reilly looked like an elegant cat-burglar in a black sweatshirt, matching slacks, and the same rope-soled sandals he had been wearing the previous day.

"Well," Luman sneered, "if it isn't the hotshot private eye! You should be working, Boyd, you don't have that much time left. Exactly?" He looked inquiringly at his redheaded associate.

Reilly consulted the small clock strapped to his wrist. "Exactly four hours and twenty-three minutes," he said in his deep baritone.

"To find out who's been hacking into the new collection," Luman continued. "I wouldn't expect you to tangle with anything in the big leagues, like murder. Leave that to a pro like Schell to figure out. A lousy amateur like you would only get under his feet."

"Watch him, Art," Reilly said with a nasty grin on his ugly face. "Any moment now he could throw his food in your face, the way he threw a martini into mine when I wasn't looking last night."

"Time is a big deal with you," I said to Luman. "Why?"

"Efficiency," he snorted. "You waste time, you waste money; things don't get done and before you know it you're on the garbage dump!"

"For sure you haven't wasted any time trying to get rid of me, almost from the moment I arrived," I said. "Maybe I'm a time-wasting factor in your campaign to make sure Freidel's new collection is a failure, so the company will lose money this year and you can buy out your other two partners for peanuts?"

Luman's face started to turn that dull red color again as his piggy little eyes glared at me viciously. "You're out of your stupid mind, Boyd! Who's been feeding you that kind of crap? Kempton, I guess? If Freidel's collection is a failure I'll lose more goddamned money that way than I'll save by buying out my partners cheap! If you can read figures, get Kempton to show you them and you'll see what I mean."

"I'll do that," I said amiably.

Reilly walked across to the cellaret and made himself a drink, then came back beside his boss and looked down at me. "You shouldn't be just sitting there, Boyd." He checked that small wrist-clock again. "Not when you've only got four hours and seventeen minutes left to find the saboteur."

His grin widened a little the moment before he threw the contents of his glass into my face. While I was trying to wipe the burning liquor out of my eyes, Reilly grabbed a fistful of my shirt and lifted me out of the chair. Then his other fist slammed into my solar plexus, making me jackknife forward from the waist. A karate chop across the back of my neck flattened me onto the floor and I just lay there helplessly.

"Nothing personal, you understand?" I heard his voice from what seemed a vast distance away. "That evens the score for last night. Nobody takes me and gets away with it, Boyd." His hands suddenly lifted me up from the floor and slammed my back into the chair I had been sitting in previously. "Maybe you should just sit for a while and think."

I opened one eye cautiously and the room stopped spinning a couple of seconds later, leaving me with only two problems; a sore neck and a stomach that felt like somebody had just put a match to it. Reilly's grinning face came into focus as he sprawled comfortably in a chair facing me.

"Get me another drink, Art," he commanded. "Somehow, I spilled the first one."

"Sure thing, Chuck." Luman waddled quickly across to the cellaret, made a fresh drink and brought it back to the redhead. Reilly took a swig from the glass, then looked at me with his eyes momentarily cold and calculating. "This is a great employer I have here," he said smoothly. "For a couple of minutes each month he lets me play boss so I won't get disenchanted, or anything."

"I wouldn't want a disenchanted associate," Luman guffawed. "It could mean I'd have to start working again."

"You know it's a ball working for you, Art," Reilly finished his drink quickly and stood up. "Don't forget, Boyd, time is running out on you real fast."

They both walked out of the room leaving me to nurse my bruised ego and intestines. A few minutes later the pain quietened down into a dull ache, so I managed to sit upright on the chair. Life as lived in

Freidel's nuthouse was never boring, I philosophized, as long as you had the stamina to stay with it. I didn't bear any grudge against Reilly, either; I merely hoped he'd turn his back on me sometime real soon when I was holding a baseball bat in my hand.

"Mr. Boyd," a throaty voice said, "I've been looking all over for you. How can you sit around doing nothing at a time like this? It's not fair to all us unprotected girls."

The blond house model, Kitty, stood framed in the doorway. Her big baby-blue eyes had a reproachful look, and her full lips were beginning to pout. She was wearing a short black robe which came about halfway down her thighs and which was tied loosely with a belt. Her legs and feet were bare. I wondered if she was wearing anything beneath the robe. Somehow I didn't think she was. I have great faith in my instincts, and my instincts at that moment were what are generally called base.

"You sick, or something?" she asked plaintively.

"Only a sudden twinge from an old bullet wound." I grinned bravely at her. "The cops told me I was stupid to go up against the three of them in that garage—all known killers with nothing to lose!—but what the hell?" I shrugged modestly. "Somebody had to do it."

Her eyes widened. "Gosh, Mr. Boyd! What happened?"

"Afterward, they figured they had four corpses to carry out, so the cops told me a long time later. But then, apparently, I opened my eyes and asked if anybody was carrying a hip flask, so they knew I wasn't dead."

"Where did the bullet hit you?"

"Bullets." I corrected her in a gentle voice. "Bugsy was using a submachine gun, and stitched a row of holes straight across my chest."

"Gosh!" she said again, and who the hell cared

about her limited vocabulary while she looked the way she did.

"They fixed me up real good in the hospital," I said. "An artificial heart, a couple of artificial lungs, seven stainless-steel ribs—"

"Mr. Boyd," she said suspiciously, "are you joshing me?"

"Gosh, Kitty, and heavens-to-Betsy, even!" I got up onto my feet carefully. "Whatever makes you think a thing like that?"

"I can tell, mostly. Anyway"—her voice became brisk—"we want to have a private talk with you in my room right now. That's why I was looking for you."

"We?"

"Deborah and me. It's very confidential."

"Okay," I said, "I guess I've got nothing to lose but my mind."

"I wouldn't worry about that." She smiled sweetly. "I'm sure that hospital can give you an artificial one, and it'll probably be an improvement."

She ran up the two flights of the staircase as if they weren't there. I followed behind her, more slowly, savoring the exciting view of her bare bottom as the robe rose up over it. My instinct had been right. She was wearing nothing beneath it. A tingle of excitement radiated out from my awakening groin. The cheeks of her bottom bounced wildly as she ran, and I just longed to get my hands on them. At the top of the stairs she turned and waited patiently for me to catch up with her. I took my time. Between her legs, I glimpsed her delta of wispy yellow hair and the slit that rose up through it.

She led the way to her room, which was next to mine and the last one at the end of the hallway. The room was neat and pleasantly furnished, and I could smell a faint perfume. The red-haired house model, Deborah, was sitting on the bed, idly swinging her legs—which, protruding from her robe, were mostly bare.

"You sure took your time," she said to Kitty. "We made a pact, remember?"

"Honest, I had to look everyplace before I found didn't do anything we should, did we, Mr. Boyd?" him." The blonde looked at me appealingly. "We "No," I grunted, then sank into the nearest chair. "Why don't the two of you call me Danny?"

"It's not much of a start, but I guess it's something." Kitty sat down on the bed beside Deborah and crossed her legs carelessly, affording me another glimpse of the creamy patch between her legs. Then she pulled the hem down over her thighs blocking off my view. I had seen quite enough. In those kind of split-second glimpses, my mind always functions like a high-speed shutter.

Deborah's gray-green eyes looked at me with a kind of calculated appraisal. "We're disappointed in you, Danny. Very disappointed, aren't we, Kitty?"

Kitty nodded vigorously. "When I finally found him in the dining room he was sitting on a chair. Just sitting! Can you imagine that, Deborah? I don't believe he was even sitting and thinking!"

"If you're trying to built up a cross-talk comic act, it needs a hell of a lot more practice yet," I growled. "Something like funny in the dialog, too."

"This isn't meant to be funny," the blonde snapped. "This is very serious, isn't it, Deborah?"

"Very," the redhead agreed. "You see, Danny, last night there were three of us, and now there are only the two of us. Somebody murdered poor Stephanie last night, or has that fact slipped your mind?"

"We can't help thinking maybe that same somebody might decide to murder one of us tonight," Kitty said. "Who is going to protect us, we asked ourselves. Not the police because they don't live here. Then Deborah said—"

"—That wonderful private detective from New York is what I said." The redhead glared at me. "The one with the darling cleft chin, who's in love with himself. That big hunk of man called Boyd, and I bet he's got the murderer in his sights already."

"And what did you say?" I snarled at the blonde.

"I said we should have a little private talk with you and make sure." She recrossed her legs, and I got that yellow flash again. Her slit was wider, and I caught sight of more shiny pink flesh. "Only now you've got us worried so I'm not even sure we'll be safe with you tonight."

"Three in the bed, we figured, with you in the middle and we could sleep happily," Deborah volunteered.

"Well, honey"—Kitty smiled softly—"we figured we could sleep finally. It sounded like a real great fun-and-safety project! Do you have the murderer in your sights already, Danny?"

"No!" I closed my eyes for a couple of seconds. "Look, if you two crazy broads figure it's simple, let me . . ." My voice trailed away into nothing because they obviously weren't listening to me. They were too busy giving each other meaningful glances.

"Shall we tell him, Kitty?"

"I guess it would only be fair, Deborah," the blonde said, "and a lot safer for us, too."

"The truth is," Deborah announced solemnly, "Flavian killed her."

"Eldridge?" My voice came out a squeak and I cleared my throat hastily. "How the hell do you figure that?"

"Stephanie told me all about it late last night," Kitty whispered. "She came into my room just before she went to bed. I mean, she left here to go to bed but who knows if Flavian was waiting for her even then? We had a real gabfest of girlish confidences while she was here."

I lit a cigarette, then held it between my fingers and watched the smoke drifting upward. It was something to do, one stage better than starting to cut out paper dolls. "Let me get his straight," I said carefully. "She told you Eldridge was going to kill her, then happily went back to her room to wait for him to come along and do it?"

"Of course not—silly!" She gave me a patronizing smile. "She told me why Flavian had been so made at her earlier in the night. You were there when they had that fight in the bar, remember? Well, it had nothing to do with her wearing the new model dress, that was only Flavian's excuse. He was scared she was about to tell Dion everything she knew, and he wanted to stop her."

"I'll ask a stupid question," I muttered. "What did she know?"

"You know something, Danny?" Deborah said in a brooding voice. "For a professional private detective, you sure are a slow starter!"

"Stephanie found out it was Flavian who'd been deliberately ruining the new collection," Kitty said. "But she couldn't make up her mind if she should tell Dion, and Flavian kept on pleading with her the whole time until she finally got to feeling a little sorry for him."

"That's why she came in here last night, to talk it over with Kitty," Deborah added helpfully. "She wanted advice."

"I said she should tell Dion in the morning, but she still wasn't too sure what she'd do when she left here." The blonde sighed mournfully. "I guess she had a soft spot someplace for that crazy little fag and look what it got her—dead!"

I mashed the butt of my cigarette in the nearest

ashtray, took a slow deep breath and tried to look both alert and intelligent. "How did she know it was Flavian who'd been ruining the dresses?"

"You remember that crazy yellow number she was wearing last night? It was one out of the collection and Lenore said for her to wear it for a while because—"

"I know!" I growled.

Kitty glared at me and lifted her chin a couple of inches higher. "Well! If you're going to interrupt me every time I—"

"I'm sorry," I whimpered. "Please go on."

"I don't think I will, now you've been so horribly rude to me." She crossed her arms under her full breasts, expanding them into some Amazonian fantasy, and almost lifting them right out of the opening of her robe, then recrossed her legs. I was getting so downhearted by the whole bit, I didn't even notice the moist yellow flash this time.

"I'll tell him." Deborah's gray-green eyes stared at me icily. "He won't dare interrupt me or I'll chew off his balls and throw them straight out the window." She waited awhile to make sure her threat had gotten home, and it gave me time to light another cigarette and hold it between my fingers while I watched the smoke—along with my mind—spiral upward into nothingness.

"Stephanie was long on height, short on memory," Deborah said. "She forgot about the dress belonging in the new collection until around nine-thirty last night. Then she remembered she'd seen Dion working late so she ran into the workroom, but he wasn't there. She figured there was still a chance he was up in the storeroom putting away the garment he'd been working on, so she rushed up the stairs and found the storeroom door was closed. But when she tried the doorknob, she found the door wasn't locked so she walked right in and"—the redhead paused for breath and dramatic effect—"found Flavian in there with a pair of shears in his hand!"

"Stephanie screamed and ran out of the room," Kitty said excitedly, "and Flavian chased after her. She ran back to her own room but before she could lock the door he'd forced his way inside. He was completely hysterical, she said; screamed and cried and begged her not to tell Dion. He even threatened to kill her if she told on him! Poor Stephanie was so confused and scared, she said she needed time to think it over. Finally Flavian calmed down a little after he made her promise to tell him her decision first. That was why he chased her into the bar last night, he figured she'd decided to tell Dion without letting him know first."

"May I"—I tried to fit a polite smile onto my lips but the corners of my mouth turned down at the last moment, so it came out a dirty sneer—"ask a couple of questions?"

"I think you should be encouraged to ask questions, Danny." Kitty gave me another of those sweet smiles. "It could mean your brain is working at long last."

"How did Flavian get inside the storeroom?" I grated.

"He told Stephanie about that in the middle of all his hysterical ravings about how he was jealous of Dion and wanted to ruin him as a designer," she answered complacently. "Apparently Dion asked his advice about locking the garments away for safety after the first sabotage happened, and Flavian suggested the storeroom because he knew there was a duplicate key, which he kept for himself."

"Freidel didn't remember that?"

Deborah laughed softly. "You don't know Dion too well, Danny. He can forget to shave the other half of his face some mornings. He only lives for two things; designing clothes, and sleeping with women. The rest, he just puts out of his mind the whole time."

"You have a second question, Danny?" Kitty purred.

"You're goddamned right I do!" I swallowed so hard I nearly choked on the apple inside my own throat. "If you knew all this from Stephanie last night, why the hell didn't you tell it to the lieutenant this morning?"

They both turned their heads and looked at each other for a while. The look that passed between them was explicit. It said men are moronic, and why do we waste our time telling them things their poor brains can't even comprehend? I gritted my teeth and waited until their heads turned in unison toward me.

"Danny," Deborah smiled wearily. "What if he hadn't believed us?"

"He would have put Eldridge through the hoops," I grated.

"And maybe finished up believing whatever Flavian said." Kitty shook her head slowly. "What we mean is, our story would only be hearsay, or whatever, and if Flavian convinced the lieutenant we were lying he would let him stay in the house." She shrugged her shoulder daintily. "You think we wanted to end up corpses before the day was out?"

Every male over the age of twelve knows better than argue with the kind of insane logic produced by the feminine mind. I opened my mouth a couple of times, then managed to shut it without saying anything.

"We discussed the whole matter very seriously," Deborah said. "At first, we figured the safest thing, if we wanted to go on living, was to say nothing. But then we thought that wouldn't be fair to poor Stephanie."

"Or Dion," Kitty added.

"So we finally decided to put our lives in your hands, Danny." Deborah grimaced suddenly. "And right now that worries me!"

"And me," Kitty nodded vehemently. "I mean, a

guy who looks handsome and virile is enough under normal circumstances."

"But in a situation like this we need a man who is also intelligent," Deborah added. "Nothing personal, Danny."

"Suppose I call Lieutenant Schell right now?" I suggested. "Then you can both tell him your story and—"

"If you call that lieutenant, we'll tell him you're out of your mind," Kitty snapped. "Dion hired you to catch the saboteur who's now become a murderer. We've just told you it's Flavian Eldridge, so that leaves you with just the easy part to do—prove it. As soon as he's behind bars, we'll both agree to testify in court if you like."

"Thanks a bunch," I said bitterly.

Kitty recrossed her legs and I registered the pale yellow flash. A couple of seconds later Deborah did the same thing, and I wasn't startled to see she wasn't wearing any pants either. Her hair was thicker than Kitty's. Right then they could have staged a private exhibition for my benefit; I wouldn't have bothered watching.

"Maybe we can recap a little?" I grinned blearily at the both of them. "Stephanie came in here and told Kitty what had happened, then left apparently to go to her bed, still undecided about telling Dion in the morning, right?"

"Right," Kitty nodded vigorously.

"Then you told Deborah about it when?"

"First thing this morning, before we heard the terrible news about poor Stephanie having been murdered."

"And you both agreed she should tell Dion?" They nodded their heads in grave unison. "I guess you're more loyal to your boss than Stephanie was?"

"He's the ultimate!" Kitty said.

"He's more than that." Deborah's voice sounded a little dreamy.

"It doesn't worry you he sleeps around the whole time?" I asked.

"What's a Libby Cathcart?" Deborah shrugged her shoulders disdainfully. "Or a Lenore Brophy, even."

Kitty giggled. "And never mind a Polly Peridot!" Her voice sounded smug. "Anyway, he always comes back to us."

"You know something?" Deborah said. "With Danny hot on Flavian's trail, I think we'll be safe with just two in a bed tonight, and the door locked from the inside, of course."

"Two in a bed, meaning you and me?" Kitty queried.

The redhead nodded, then gave me a long speculative look. "I definitely think we should save the three in a bed idea—"

"Don't forget it's Danny in the middle," the blonde interjected.

"—until after Danny's proved Flavian killed poor Stephanie and he's safely locked away behind bars," Deborah finished.

Kitty beamed at me. "It would be a lovely reward."

"A night to remember always." Deborah slowly licked her bottom lip. "So—go to it, Danny Boyd!"

"Either one of us, alone, is the answer to any man's dream of paradise," Kitty gurgled. "Imagine how it will be with the two of us, together! What are you waiting for, Danny Boyd?"

I got out of the chair and headed toward the doorway, wondering what in hell I had done with my mind. For sure, I vaguely remembered, I'd had it with me when I first walked into the room.

Chapter SIX

Reassurance was what I needed right then; the feel of grass under my feet and the sky over my head, so I knew the rest of the world still had some kind of sanity left. I went out of the house and walked around the perimeter of the grounds, skirting the high electrified fence, until I finally arrived back at the pool. The westering sun made the surface of the water a shimmering golden lake which looked inviting, until I remembered what had happened in the early hours of the morning. The thought made the drink-wagon look even more inviting, so I made myself a drink and relaxed in one of the reclining chairs. Around five minutes later I heard footsteps coming toward me, turned my head and saw Kempton approaching with a nervous smile on his face.

"I was hoping I might find you, Mr. Boyd." His magnified eyes in back of the thick lens held a pleading look. "What a dreadful day it's been! That girl, Stephanie, being murdered, and then the police lieutenant asking all those questions. Schell is an old friend of mine, as I told you last night, but he seemed a complete stranger when he was questioning me."

"To a cop," I said, "a friend is a guy you beat up with a rubber hose, instead of a nightstick."

The magnified eyes widened. "You don't think they really use—"

"I was just kidding," I told him.

He fiddled around making himself a drink. "If you don't mind my asking, Mr. Boyd, have you made any progress?"

"I never met so many nuts under one roof before," I admitted. "Give it another twenty-four hours and I'll be ready for a restrainer. Except that"—I checked my watch "according to Luman I've only got around another three hours to come up with the answer, or he tosses me out on my ear. To be precise, I guess Reilly will do the tossing. Luman says you're a liar, incidentally."

"What?" Kempton sounded shocked.

"He says if the new collection is a failure he'll lose more money than he'd save by being able to buy you and Freidel out cheap. If you can read figures, he told me, get Kempton to show you them."

"I'll be happy to show you the figures anytime, Mr. Boyd, but I assure you what Luman says just isn't true. If the new collection does fail, it will only mean a short-term loss. The savings effected by removing both Dion and myself from a partnership interest would more than compensate for the trading loss. In fact, over the following two years it would have to show Luman an enormous profit."

"Suppose he does get rid of the both of you? How does he keep the company going without Freidel, the designer?" I asked curiously.

"There are other alternatives open to Luman." Kempton sipped his drink, the look on his face said it was something the doctor had prescribed to keep him unhappy. "He would still own the Freidel label, and could easily employ another designer. Or even engage Dion to continue designing on a salary basis."

"Polly Peridot told me she gave Dion his start?"

He nodded. "Quite correct, Mr. Boyd. She—uh—kept him until he had enough work done to prove himself. Then she brought him to me, and I was sufficiently impressed to think of a partnership. But, as you know, the only place we could raise enough capital was from Luman."

"In the beginning, Freidel had the talent, you had the money—right?" I said.

"Perfectly correct," he nodded again.

"You've got Luman set up as the villain; the guy who figures he's got a chance to buy out both his partners cheap, and will stop at nothing to do it. Did you ever think that, out of the three partners, you're the one who is most expendable, Mr. Kempton?"

He removed his glasses, rubbed his eyes vigorously, then pushed the heavy black-framed lens back into place. "What are you getting at, Mr. Boyd?"

"Maybe Luman isn't the only villain." I said. "Maybe he and Freidel are working together in this, to get rid of you. It would be easy for them to take over the manufacturing and distribution setup you've already established. Then, with you out of the way, Freidel could come up with a brilliant new collection to wipe out his previous failure and they could split the profit right down the middle."

"I couldn't believe that of Dion!" Kempton swallowed painfully. "He's not only my partner, he's my friend."

"What's a friend where money is concerned?" I sneered. "When the sabotage of the new collection started, you suggested hiring a professional to deal with it and Schell recommended me. How did Freidel react to the suggestion?"

"Well," he floundered for a moment, "I'll admit he wasn't exactly enthusiastic; said he thought it was somebody's idea of a practical joke. But when it kept on happening, I pressed the point and he finally agreed it would be a logical answer."

"Why don't we go talk to him about it?" I said easily.

"Eh?" A look of panic showed on his face. "I couldn't possibly do that, Mr. Boyd! It's unthinkable!

You couldn't reasonably expect me to go and accuse Dion—my partner and friend—of cheating me?"

"I don't," I told him. "But there's no reason why I can't accuse him of just that, is there?"

He brushed his hands through his thinning hair, and I noticed his fingers were trembling slightly. "I suppose I can't stop you from doing anything you think is necessary, Mr. Boyd. I'll just wait here and—"

"I want you there," I snapped. "You don't have to take any part in the conversation. In fact, you can be horrified at my suggestion, if you want. But I figure you should see Freidel's—and Luman's—reaction to the idea."

"Very well," he quavered, "if you absolutely insist on me being there. I warn you, Mr. Boyd, I won't back your accusation at all."

"I guess it would be out of character if you did," I grunted, "like a sheep snapping at a wolf. Do something for me? Go back to the house and round up Freidel, Luman, and Eldridge, and get them together in Freidel's workroom. I'll be there in ten minutes."

"All right, but why Eldridge?" He blinked at me uncertainly. "What has he got to do with all this?"

"That's what I want to find out," I said amiably.

He turned around and started toward the house, dragging his feet, his rear view looking about as enthusiastic as his face had a few moments before. I made myself another drink, then suddenly my mind proved its photographic retention by triggering off a couple of subliminal pictures—a pale-yellow flash, followed by a red flash which proved beyond doubt that Deborah was a natural redhead. I sternly banished both pictures from my mind because I knew if I allowed them to stay any longer I would start right in building a cage. Then, after I had locked Eldridge inside so I could prove he was behind bars, I would rush off and collect my reward. The two of them would make a nice contrast, with one Danny Boyd sandwiched in the middle, taking things as they came.

Five minutes later I put my empty glass down on the drink-wagon and went back to the house. They were all there in the workroom, waiting for me when I walked in: Kempton looking even more worried than he had ten minutes back; Freidel sitting on the end of the workbench, idly swinging his legs, his face bland. Luman had a look of petulant impatience on his face, while Reilly lounged in back of him with a derisive grin curling his lips. Eldridge looked like the last of the Oscar Wilde set in a sky-blue silk shirt with an enormous floppy collar, and a pair of skintight off-white pants; the thick belt was composed of alternate red-white-and-blue vertical stripes and the buckle was made of polished brass. Looking at them in turn, I got the uneasy feeling that none of them, except maybe Kempton, was for real and any moment now I would wake up in Manhattan with a lousy hangover.

"Everyone is here as you requested, Mr. Boyd." Kempton smiled uncertainly at Freidel. "I don't know what this is all about, of course, but as Mr. Boyd said it was important I—"

"Shut up," Luman grunted. "It's his party, let him tell it!"

"Don't be too hard on Harry," Freidel said in a mild voice. "You know you make him nervous, Art."

Luman looked at Reilly, who pointedly looked at the small clock strapped to his wrist, and the fat man nodded agreement. "We're wasting time. If you've got anything to say, Boyd, say it!"

"I was hired to find out who was sabotaging Dion's new collection, and stop it," I said. "Then there was an extra problem of murder that came up this morning. Obviously, the two are connected. So you can't solve one problem without also solving the other."

"It sounds like a line from a song someplace," Reilly chuckled.

"So first, you have to look for motivation," I continued. "Who stands to gain if the new collection is a failure? We know you do"—I nodded toward the fat man—"because you can buy out both your partners cheap if the company has a loss in any financial year. According to Mr. Kempton the failure would only be a short-term loss, more than compensated for by the savings you'd make with the other two removed from a partnership interest. In fact, Mr. Kempton claims, you'd show an enormous profit over the next couple of years."

Luman's small eyes sunk in the rolls of fat glittered balefully as he glared at Kempton. "Is that what you told him, Harry?" he rasped.

"Well," Kempton said in a shaking voice, "the questions were all Mr. Boyd's idea, Art, you understand? I just gave him the facts."

"So the first real motive is financial," I said to Luman. "You could have installed yourself and your—uh—associate, inside this house to deliberately prevent the new collection being a success. It's failure would give you the chance to get rid of both your partners, or maybe just one of them."

"What the hell are you talking about now?" Luman demanded, a baffled look on his face.

I expounded the theory for a second time that Kempton was the most expendable of the three partners. So maybe Luman and Freidel had gotten together to get ird of good old Harry, then later Freidel could come up with a brilliant new collection and they would have it made.

"I guess I shouldn't have hit him so hard," Reilly said reflectively. "But how the hell was I to know Boyd carries his brains around in his belly?"

"You're wrong, Danny," Freidel snapped. "You

think I'd work myself into the ground the way I have over the last few months designing this collection, then turn around and happily ruin it?"

"I wouldn't know," I told him. "How important is money to you, Dion? Just how valuable is this sultan's style of living you've become accustomed to, with its inbuilt harem, and all?"

He gave me a long icy stare, then shrugged his shoulders and turned toward Kempton. "Harry, you can't believe I'd do something like that to you. You're the guy who made everything possible for me. We've not only been partners, but also good friends over the last few years. Believe me, I'd prefer to give Art my share of the goddamned company for free than double-cross you!"

"I know, Dion, I know!" Kempton looked like he was about to bust out crying any moment. "This whole idea is Boyd's, not mine."

"I guess that's right." Freidel carefully brushed his moustache with his index finger, then grinned bleakly at me. "You got any more lousy theories, Danny?"

"Just the one," I said. "If Art was determined on getting rid of both his partners, he'd need help from inside this house. Somebody on your permanent staff who knew your work, and could function as an effective saboteur because they also had access to it."

"I'm getting awful tired of this," Luman snarled. "Any minute now I'm going to tell Chuck to kick your teeth in, Boyd!"

"It would be a kindness," Reilly said easily. "The way he runs off at the mouth the whole time, a few teeth down his throat would keep his voice blocked and give us all a break."

"Take it easy, Art," Freidel snapped. "Suddenly I want to hear the rest of this."

"You pick the right person and you offer them an irresistible bribe," I said. "You say, help me get rid of both my partners and you'll have the chance to become a great fashion designer working for me. Or do you want to spend the rest of your life just a lousy assistant, with your own genius for design being throttled the whole time by that lousy bastard Freidel!" I waited for the inevitable explosion and it came a split-second later.

"It's a lie!" Eldridge shrieked. "A dirty stinking lie! You know I'd never do a dreadful thing like that, Dion. I couldn't."

"Don't get hysterical, Flavian," Freidel said drily. "This is only a theory." He looked at me quickly. "Or is it, Danny?"

"You remember who had the bright idea of locking away the garments you'd been working on during the day in the storeroom each night?" I asked him.

His heavy eyebrows knit as he concentrated, making his face more satanic-looking than ever. "I remember," he said finally, "it was Flavian."

"I wonder if he knew there was a duplicate key to the storeroom, and where to find it?" I said.

"I don't know anything about a duplicate key!" Eldridge sounded like he was on the verge of tears. "I only suggested the storeroom because it seemed the safest place. All this is some horrible plot of Boyd's to blame me for what's happened, because he thinks I'm the easiest one to railroad! You know I've always been loyal to you, Dion, always! I'd cut off my right hand before I'd do anything to hurt you."

Freidel still watched my face carefully, ignoring Eldridge completely. "I'm not sure if there is a duplicate key," he said in an expressionless voice. "It's possible."

"Stephanie forgot to return that yellow dress to you last night so you could lock it away with the rest of the stuff," I said. "She knew you had been working late and when she found you'd left the workroom, she could have figured there was a chance you were in the storeroom. Maybe she went up there and found Eldridge instead—with a pair of cutting shears in his hand—all set to go. She would have run, of course, probably back to her own room with Eldridge right in back of her. He would have pleaded and threatened to try and make her keep her mouth shut. That could explain the scene in the bar last night when he came chasing after her, figuring she was about to tell you what she knew. He was prepared to do anything to stop her from talking; even tried to pull the dress right off her, remember? She was so mad at him she hit him but then, when she had the chance, she didn't tell you. So he didn't have to worry anymore, he could just sit in an armchair and make idle chitchat about how he was dying from the punch in the nose she gave him."

"Let me understand this, Danny," Freidel said in a harsh voice. "You figure he changed his mind later, decided he couldn't trust Stephanie to keep her mouth shut, so he killed her?"

"Using the shears he'd taken from Lenore's workbench earlier in the evening to use in his cut-up caper," I said. "He returned them to the top drawer of her workbench after he'd murdered Stephanie. I was there this morning when Lenore found them. The police have them now, of course."

"Dion!" Eldridge hurtled across the room and threw himself down on his knees in front of the designer. "I swear I never killed Stephanie! It's all foul horrible lies. I don't know why Boyd hates me so much, he's invented that crazy story, but you know I worship you, Dion. I always have! Your great genius for design, your inspirational—" The back of Freidel's hand across his mouth suddenly reduced him to a whimpering silence.

Freidel slid off the edge of the workbench onto his feet, grabbed a handful of Eldridge's silk shirt and hauled him upright. "All right," he said softly, "if you didn't kill Stephanie, then who did?"

"One of the other two house models," Eldridge gurgled frantically. "I've told you that all along. You've always figured them as three frames to hang clothes on, or just sexual objects available for your use anytime you wanted them. But the three of them were intelligent girls, Dion, and they reacted with all the bitchery any woman is capable of when she's been rejected. They didn't mind sharing you among them, but when you gave them the brush-off and started sleeping around with other women like Lenore and Libby Cathcart, they hated you. They thought they would punish you by ruining the new collection." He shook the light brown hair out of his eyes with a convulsive swing of his head, while his voice climbed higher into the treble range. "Don't you see what happened last night? For some reason Stephanie changed her mind about you, and was stupid enough to tell those other two bitches. Kitty and Deborah knew if she confessed to you what they'd done, that would finish their chances of ever getting you back. Anything was better than that, including murder!"

Freidel slowly relaxed his grip on Eldridge's silk shirt, then gave him an impatient shove which sent him skittering backward across the room. His dark eyes had an opaque look in them as he stared at me. "How about that, Danny?" he whispered.

"It's neat," I conceded. "It not only takes Flavian off the hook, it does the same for Art, too."

"Maybe Boyd has real proof, instead of all these wonderful theories," Reilly said in a bored voice. "Like he could have found that duplicate key in Flavian's room, or maybe saw him put those shears back into Lenore's workroom?"

"No proof," I grated.

"How about you, Flavian?" He looked across at

Eldridge who was cringing against the far wall, the back of his hand pressed against his mouth. "You got any proof it was one, or both, of those girls who killed Stephanie?"

"I don't have any proof," Eldridge whimpered. "I just know it's true!" He took his hand away from his mouth and his eyes widened in horror as he saw the few glistening drops of blood on his knuckles.

"You pay your nickel and you gets your choice!" Reilly shrugged.

"Goddamned right!" Luman snorted. "Anybody want to bet the next time around Boyd will give us a great story about how the girl was Goldilocks in disguise—wearing a black wig—and that's why the bears killed her? He won't have any proof, of course, just another goddamned theory!"

"I think, Danny," Freidel said coldly, "from here on out it could be a good idea if you keep your mouth shut until you've got something tangible to back up what you say." He turned his back on me, then slammed his fist down on the top of the workbench. "If I don't get back to work, this collection will never be finished on time. So will everybody please get the hell out of here?"

Kempton scuttled out of the door fast, giving a kind of weird impersonation of an elderly crab on the lam. Eldridge followed him, licking his knuckles, his eyes still horrified at the sight of his own blood. Then Luman waddled past me like I wasn't there, but his associate stopped beside me.

"I was real glad to see you give it a try, even if you did strike out." He rubbed the tip of his hooked nose gently and showed his crooked teeth in a wide grin. "Time's running out on you real fast, Boyd." He made a production out of checking that strap-clock on his wrist. "You've only got two hours and sixteen minutes left!"

"I like you, Chuck—old buddy!—about the same way you like me," I growled. "Out by the pool last night maybe I did jump you when you kind of weren't looking. You did the same to me in the dining room a couple of hours back, so that makes us even. But nobody is about to get tossed out of this house on their ear tonight."

"Who says they're not?"

"Lieutenant Schell," I said flatly. "Nobody is leaving until he's solved his homicide case."

The grin faded abruptly from his face. "I'd forgotten about that." He rubbed the tip of his nose more vigorously. "I guess we'll just have to get along for a while."

"Fine," I said. "Don't forget to tell your associate, huh?"

"I'll tell my boss," he snapped. "I'm Mr. Luman's associate, remember?"

"You sure could have fooled me." I grinned at him. "The way the both of you act when you're together, I would have figured you were the boss."

"You figured wrong, like always," he snarled.

"I guess I just wasn't observant enough," I said apologetically. "I'll be sure and watch the both of you together real close in future so I can figure out where I made the mistake."

The red glint showed up in his eyes for a moment, then vanished again. "You shouldn't push your nose too far, Boyd. You never know when you can get it chopped off, like at the back of your neck!"

"Look who's talking about noses?" I sneered.

He held down his temper the way he had beside the pool, visibly sweating with the effort. "I've got a theory that Freidel and Kempton got together and hired you," he rasped. "Not to find out who was messing up their new designs, but to see if you could hang something on Art that would force him out of the partnership, and they didn't care how you did it."

"It beats Luman's theory about Goldilocks, anyway," I said mildly.

"And if I prove it to my own satisfaction," he went on in a lowered voice, so Freidel couldn't hear him, "I'm going to fix your wagon permanently, Boyd. Like put a hole"—the spatulate tip of his index finger tapped the bridge of my nose sharply—"right there!"

Chapter SEVEN

I went up to my room, showered, and put on my new suit; a tropic-weight that had set me back a couple of hundred bucks, and the color was Jamaican blue. So I was in California, not Jamaica, but how the hell could the suit know that? The phone rang while I was checking out the profile in the mirror and I felt my scalp twitch irritably. I was dead right, nothing should disturb the sacred moments. The butler's fruity voice told me Lieutenant Schell was calling and I heard the familiar rasping voice a few seconds later.

"Made any progress since this morning, Boyd?"

"No," I said truthfully. "How about you?"

"A big fat zero! The cutting shears checked out as the murder weapon okay, but there were no prints. I figure the Brophy girl was right when she said anybody could have taken them from her workbench during the night. Besides, if she was the killer, she wouldn't have been that stupid to put them back into the top drawer!"

"I guess not," I said. "Any word on Luman from L.A.?"

"Another zero. They say he's a nothing; a penny-ante wheeler and dealer who just doesn't rate. No record, either."

"Maybe you should get them to check out Reilly."

"Reilly?" An anxious bark came into his voice. "But he's just Luman's stooge, isn't he?"

"I'm not too sure," I said carefully. "Watching the both of them together, I sometimes get the feeling it's the other way about."

"Okay, I'll get them to run a check on him. Anything else?"

I figured one bone a day was more than enough for a hound like Schell. "Not at the moment, Lieutenant."

"You get onto anything, Boyd, anything at all, you call me!"

"Sure," I said. "Us unsworn deputies know our duty, Lieutenant!"

He said something under his breath, then slammed the phone down in my ear. My watch said it was five of seven, and my stomach said now was a good time to have a drink and cleanse the taste of Schell out of my system. I figured there was no point in wasting my own private bottle when there were all those bottles still unused in the bar downstairs. As I walked down the hallway, I saw Libby Cathcart standing at the head of the stairs.

She was wearing an embroidered shift that must have been a steal at five hundred bucks. Against the light, I could see her body outlined beneath it. It was trim and firm. There was no sag to her breasts as far as I could see. Her long black hair had been brushed back over her ears and tied in a loose knot at the back of her head.

"What a pleasant coincidence, Mr. Boyd," she said in that nicely-modulated soprano. "I was just about to look for you. Can you spare me a few minutes?"

"Sure," I said. "How about joining me in the bar, I was headed that way."

"I'd prefer we talk privately in my room." She thought about it for a moment, then gave me a tentative smile. "I'm sure I can find you a drink there."

"It gets so complicated when you can't remember where you hid the last fifth," I said sympathetically. "Have you looked under the bed lately?"

Her face frosted over as she turned away from me and started toward her room at the other side of the stairway. I followed a couple of paces in back of her, like a humble retainer should, and when we got inside she closed the door. Her room was a guestroom the way mine was, but there the resemblance came to an abrupt halt. Her room was about four times the size of mine and elaborately decorated in gold and white. The furniture was all spindly-legged and intricately carved, dominated by an enormous four-poster bed. She opened up a small cellaret from the wall, then looked at me inquiringly. "I seem to have both Scotch and bourbon, Mr. Boyd."

"I'd like that," I told her.

Her mouth tightened. "Polly Peridot was wrong as usual when she said you were a humorist. I find you most unfunny, Mr. Boyd, and abominably rude!"

"So long as you don't backhand me across the face the way you did Polly." I shrugged. "Okay! I guess it's your Fifth Avenue plus five million dollars—inherited, of course—outlook on life that bugs me a little. But it wasn't your fault you were born in Tiffany's front window. I'll have bourbon, thanks."

Her smile looked genuine as she busied herself making the drinks. "Please sit down, Mr. Boyd, and you're right about the inherited money. My grandfather was the bastard son of a man who owned a number of steel mills, and my grandmother used to work for free on her rest-day in the whorehouse because she had a vocation. My father had a rich inheritance and was brought up to be a gentleman, so he wasn't interested in money because he didn't need it. Fortunately, he had the good sense to marry my mother who also had a rich inheritance. They had a fruitful but thankfully short life together until they were both killed in an automobile accident when I was twelve years old. He spent his time trying to translate Shakespeare into Urdu, or something equally ridiculous because he had no flair for languages at all. My mother spent most of her time sleeping with the servants. Even when I was quite small, I used to think of them in terms of the 'Wednesday footman,' and the 'Friday chauffeur.' I can still remember the strong sense of grateful relief when my uncle arrived to break the news that they were both dead."

She sat down beside me on the awkward-looking couch and handed me a drink. "I'd never dream of talking like this in New York, or anywhere on the East Coast for that matter, but California doesn't count somehow. Besides, you've already told me you live on the wrong side of the park so it's most unlikely we would ever meet socially. I just wanted to reassure you that your immediate ancestors were probably far more worthy than mine, so you have no need to feel inferior. You are, of course, infinitely inferior to me, Mr. Boyd, but as I said before it's not important in California."

"I can understand how Freidel gets a kick out of leaping into your bed," I said admiringly. "Or does he have to wait for the word of command, then crawl in feet-first?"

"Don't take refuge in vulgarity, Mr. Boyd. If you can't do better than that, I'll be disappointed in you." Her dark slumberous eyes held a mocking glint in them as she looked at me. "Dion has already sadly disappointed me by showing a preference for that gawky blonde he has working for him. That's what I want to talk with you about."

"Lenore Brophy?" I queried.

"I believe that's her name." Her nails beat a faint tattoo against the side of her glass for a couple of seconds. "I need some advice, Mr. Boyd. Professional advice, and I understand you're a private detective, even if you are wearing a passable suit."

"You must give me your Manhattan address," I said. "So I can come and throw stones through your windows sometime."

"I was hoping that gauche lieutenant might have exchanged some professional confidences with you."

"Like what?"

"The time when that model was killed last night, for example?"

"Between two and three A.M. this morning," I told her. "Why?"

"It would have been a little embarrassing for me to confide in the lieutenant," she said casually. "But with you it's different because—ridiculous as the situation is!—we have been introduced and we're both guests in the same house. Last night I had a tryst with Dion. He was coming here to my room late, when everyone else was asleep. I was sitting at the dresser waiting for him, a little before one o'clock, I think. Then the door suddenly opened and that gawky blonde walked straight in here without even knocking. She said she just wanted to save me an embarrassment by letting me know she was on her way to spend the night in Dion's room. It didn't worry me in the slightest—not then, anyway—I thought that Dion had probably given her a tumble sometime over her workbench, or somewhere equally sordid, and she was jealous. But I began to feel a little disturbed as the time wore on and there was no sign of Dion. Finally, I decided to make sure, in case there was a remote chance that quaint girl had been telling the truth. Dion's room is right next door, so I went in there to check."

"And?" I dutifully prompted.

"Found it empty." She finished her drink, got up from the couch and walked over to the cellaret. "I'm not sure of the exact time but it must have been after two o'clock because I remember the last time I checked my watch was a few minutes before I went to his room, and it was almost two then."

"Maybe he was with the gawky blonde in her room?" I grunted.

"I don't think so." She came back to the couch and settled herself down again. "When I saw her this morning at breakfast I watched her quite closely. She looked at Dion, then at me, and the fury in her eyes was very obvious. If Dion had spent the night in her room she would have been dying to let me know! Women have a very primitive reaction among themselves about a thing like that."

"So what does it prove?" I shrugged. "That Freidel wasn't in his room at two A.M."

"Around the time the model was murdered," she added softly. "What did darling Polly tell you about me?"

"How do you know she even mentioned you?" I asked.

"I know Polly," she said smugly.

"Something liked you hoped Freidel's new collection will fail, so then he'd have to marry you for your money. And you'd adore to have a tame genius for a husband so you could make him design for you alone."

"Polly always did have a strong streak of practicality." Libby Cathcart's tone of voice was almost respectful. "But I've changed my mind after last night. I still hope his new collection is a miserable failure, of course, and I'll do my very bitchy best to help it along the road to disaster. But I'm not sure I want to pick up the Dion pieces afterward. It would give me an uneasy feeling, being married to a man who could be a murderer. Even if I did have the servants chain him up every night."

"Is that all you wanted to talk with me about?" I asked in a bored voice.

"There was something else." Her eyes looked darker and more slumberous-looking, as they watched me over the rim of her glass. "I had this sudden compelling urge and now, of course, Dion is permanently past tense. Then I remembered vulgarly virile you."

"Urge?" I stared at her blankly. "For what?"

"Sex." Her voice sounded so polite and remote, it effectively neutered the word.

"With me—now?" I gurgled.

"Does the thought of sex before dinner offend your blue coverall mind, Mr. Boyd?" she asked icily.

"Sex at any time is a great idea," I told her, "but with you? The idea isn't offensive, it's almost hysterically funny!"

"Funny?" Her mouth tightened into a straight line. "Why funny?"

"Making love with you would be like"—I floundered for a moment then remembered her phrase about her father—"trying to translate Shakespeare into Urdu, or something equally ridiculous."

"Ridiculous!" Her face flushed a pale pink color. "We'll find out just how ridiculous it is!"

She got up from the couch, took the half-full glass from my hand, and put it down next to her own, which I noticed was empty. Then she locked the door, came back into the center of the room, and kicked off her sandals. She reached down to the hem of her shift and in one quick movement pulled it up over her head and tossed it to one side. She turned to me, put her hands on her hips, and bared her teeth in a tigerish smile. "Some kind of a sexual joke, am I?" she said in a low, dangerous voice. "Why don't you split your sides laughing, Mr. Boyd?"

The only thing she was wearing was a pair of black briefs so small that they were no larger than a pocket handkerchief. They were caught up slightly in her crotch. The tips of her breasts were large, like shell-caps, and the brown nipples pointed at me defiantly.

"It doesn't amuse you, Mr. Boyd?" She raised her eyebrows in apparent surprise.

I didn't trust myself to speak. All I could do was dumbly shake my head and hope I wasn't acting too much like a gawky schoolkid. I had a powerful impulse to walk over and grab her, tear off her briefs, and bend her forward over the back of the couch, but I was scared to get off the couch in case I became an inadvertent Toulouse-Lautrec and found myself walking across the floor on my knees.

"Not even a smile, Mr. Boyd?" Her voice was languid.

That sudden compelling urge she had mentioned before exploded inside me. I was fully aroused, as I knew the woman standing so tantalizingly in front of me was aroused. I came off the couch in a flying leap, and before she could back away at the onslaught of an aroused maniac, I grabbed her in my arms. She came willingly, pressing her body and thighs fiercely against mine. Her breasts squashed against my chest, and my hands ran down to the waistband of her briefs, my fingers pushing them down over her buttocks. My fingers dug into her cheeks, and she ground her pelvis savagely against me, pushing my blood-engorged rod hard back against my stomach. She sank her teeth into my lower lip and I gripped the taut cheeks of her bottom even harder. Her teeth let go my lower lip and she pulled her head away, her dark eyes triumphant.

"Why, Mr. Boyd." Her voice was a caress. "I never suspected you had this strong sense of humor."

"Under the circumstances," I said, "don't you think you should call me Danny?"

"I couldn't do that, Mr. Boyd," she murmured, her fingers busily unbuttoning the front of my shirt. "My social position only allows that kind of familiarity with bellhops."

"Your social position is about to become horizontal," I told her. "Unless you've got some other positions you would prefer."

"Oh, I've got plenty." Her hand was gently massaging my chest and stomach, moving steadily downward.

"I bet you have."

She sat on the four-poster bed and waited while I stripped off my clothes, like the last one to become a nudist had to forfeit his sex life.

"Do hurry, Mr. Boyd," she said impatiently. "I can hardly wait to make a few private investigations of my own."

Then, with my clothes in an untidy heap on the floor behind me, I moved across to her, my alert stem quivering in the air between us like a pointer dog on the scent. Libby Cathcart had removed her briefs, and beneath the neat tangle of pubic hair, her open slit was like a pink gash. She reached up and took hold of my straining, twitching log.

"I like it," she said sleepily. "It's worthy of any bellhop."

Still holding on to me, she lowered her head and closed her lips around the bulbous head of my prick. Her lips were cool and moist. She knew what she was doing. Her tongue played along the underside of the glans while the fingers of her other hand gently played with my balls. Sensation was on the move. When I couldn't stand it any longer, I pushed her back across the bed and, pulling her legs apart, prepared to enter her. She stopped me.

"What's the hurry?" she whispered. "There's plenty of time."

There was, and she showed me just how experienced she was. Soon time had lost all meaning. Every movement of her tongue, her fingers, the moist feel of her pussy against my body, plumbed new depths of sensation. She manipulated me, bringing me right to the point of release, which with excellent timing she seemed to sense. Then we would rest awhile until the danger was past. Her legs and arms entwined, and her breasts filled my mouth. My fingers probed into the fleshy flaps and touched her clitoris. She held my head down between her legs while I tasted the salt on my lips and tongue, and bits of hair lodged between my teeth.

Then we were making love on the bed, our movements violent and quick. She was moaning in my ear and everything was a red haze before my eyes. I gripped the backs of her thighs and her legs were clamped tightly around my neck. I moved smoothly inside her as her body bucked and rocked beneath me. We rippled and strained in perfect harmony, and when it came, our climax was simultaneous. She gave a sharp cry as my life-force began to pump into her.

That was the first time we made love. The second time, after I had recovered my strength, was over the back of the couch, with her buttocks pointing up to me, and it was every bit as good as the time before.

Maybe an hour later I stood in front of the dresser mirror knotting my tie, and feeling a distinct empathy with the guy who reaped a whirlwind. Libby Cathcart sauntered out of the bathroom, idly toweling the underswell of her left breast.

"Mr. Boyd!" she said in mock horror. "Don't tell me you're vulgar enough to make love, then run?"

"This may come as a shock to you, Miss Cathcart," I said soberly, "but I'm hungry."

"At least you could straighten up the bed before you go." She wrinkled her nose distastefully. "It looks like a couple of bearcats were turned loose in it!"

"You're the one with a gift for a phrase," I acknowledged. "Don't tell me you forgot to pack a couple of pop-up maids?"

"I know there's one pooped-out maid here, anyway." She pummeled a cushion more or less back into shape, then flopped onto the bed. "I think I'll just curl up with my memories for a while."

I went over to the cellaret and made myself a drink, then looked at her. She was lying on her back, her hands clasped behind her neck; both knees were bent and one leg was very carelessly crossed over the other.

"From where I'm standing it would make a great picture," I said admiring. "I can see it now in one of the Sunday color supplements, captioned, 'The essential socialite.' Then the first paragraph starts, quote, Everything I am, I owe to my grandmother, unquote."

She laughed. It was the first time I had heard her do that, and it was a pleasant husky sound. "I'll have to introduce you to Uncle Vaughn when we get back to New York. He believes the West Side is that place the cab goes through when you're on your way to catch a boat to Europe."

The rye tasted good, sharpening up the anticipation of my empty stomach. I finished it in three gulps and returned the empty glass to the cellaret. "Well, thanks for everything, Miss Cathcart. I've been to some surprise parties in my time, but yours was the greatest."

"No need for thanks, Mr. Boyd," she drawled. "It comes under the heading of social research—giving help to the needy—something like that? I doubt I shall remember your name in a couple of days time." She came up into a sitting position and crossed her legs in a semi-yoga posture. "I've been thinking about last night."

"Sometimes I catch myself thinking about a day two whole months back," I said helpfully.

"I'm just trying to help you in your sordid profession," she snapped. "I can't help wondering if Dion deliberately sent that gawky blonde in here?"

"For why?"

"Because he hoped I'd be so furious with him I'd lock my door and go to sleep. That way, he'd have an alibi if he needed it. He could say the blonde spent the night in his room and nobody would know the difference, if I hadn't checked and found his room empty."

"You're supposing a whole bunch of things there," I

said. "It wouldn't stand up unless Lenore Brophy went along with it and, if she did, it means the both of them needed an alibi. For what?"

"The murder of the model," she said promptly, "what else."

"Why would Dion want to murder Stephanie?"

"You're supposed to be the detective, you find out!" She stretched out on her back again, then rolled over onto her stomach and buried her face in the cushion. "Close the door quietly on your way, Mr. Boyd."

I took a last lingering look at her small, but nicely-rounded bottom, then realize all that mind-over-matter crap might work sometimes but what I was contemplating right then was impossible. So I closed the door quietly in back of me on the way out, and headed toward the stairs.

The dining room was deserted when I walked in, except for the butler. I ordered an enormous steak—bloody—and had just finished a cigarette when it arrived. By the time I had reached the coffee stage I was feeling just fine, full of rude health in fact, and remembering how Libby Cathcart performed in bed, that seemed an appropriate phrase. I gave the butler a polite thank you on the way out of the room, then stopped for a moment.

"How long have you been working for Mr. Freidel, Sims?"

"About two years, sir."

"Were all his staff already here when you first arrived?"

"Oh, no, sir." He shook his head slowly. "There was just Mr. Freidel, and Mr. Eldridge, in those days. Miss Brophy arrived about six months later."

"How about the house models?"

"Miss Stephanie was the first, I believe, sir. She took up residence a year back. Miss Kitty and Miss Deborah came three or four months later."

"If you had to pick Miss Stephanie's murderer," I said easily, "who would you chose?"

"It would be most improper for me to do any such thing, sir!" His face was frozen with shock. "Most improper!"

"A butler gets more chance than anybody else to see what's going on inside the house," I prodded. "I'm not just gossiping for the hell of it, Sims! I'm trying to catch a murderer."

"I understand, sir." His face thawed a little. "But it would be impossible for me to say. Of course, you're right when you say a butler can't help noticing little things here and there."

I fought back a sudden urge to take his nose between my fingers and squeeze it painfully. "Little things like what?"

"Well"—his voice dropped to a confidential whisper—"the day Miss Peridot arrived she seemed to be very bright and happy, but when she saw Miss Cathcart arrive the following day she changed completely. To be honest, sir, I don't think she's been sober since."

"Is that a fact?" I mentally crossed my fingers that the self-important gleam in his eyes meant he was just warming up. "Anything more?"

"Well, I did hear one of the maids say that Miss Brophy's bed hadn't been slept in last night, but then in this house"—he coughed discreetly—"that's not unusual, if you see what I mean?"

"I do, indeed, Sims," I gave him my solemn assurance, like we were both men of the world and it wouldn't surprise us if people went and slept in other people's beds with the idea of making love, even.

"I don't think there's anything more, not that I can recollect at the moment, sir. Oh, yes. Perhaps a small matter of interest? Mr. Reilly keeps a gun in his bureau drawer"—this time he permitted himself a small grin—"the same way you do, sir!"

"Just the two of us?" I grinned back at him.

"As far as I know, sir. Mr. Freidel always has kept a gun in his room, of course."

"He's scared some bankrupt husband might get past the guards on the gates?"

"I'm sure I don't know, sir." His face was wooden again.

"Thanks, Sims, you've been a big help," I lied.

"Anytime, sir." He shook his head ponderously. "We were all fond of Miss Stephanie. She was a very hard worker, and we admired her for it. Not like the other two girls at all. They've always thought of themselves as just models, and that's all they'd ever do. But during these past few weeks, Miss Stephanie was working twelve hours a day, and more sometimes. If it hadn't been for her help, I don't honestly think Mr. Eldridge would have got everything finished for the new showing in time."

"Mr. Eldridge?" I queried.

He blinked twice. "Sorry, sir. Slip of the tongue! I meant, Mr. Freidel, of course."

Chapter EIGHT

I met the red-haired house model in the doorway of the bar. She was still wearing the robe I had seen her in earlier, open at the front to show the deep plunge of her boobs.

"Danny!" She gave me a warm smile. "I've been looking for you all over! Where have you been the last couple of hours?"

"Around," I said vaguely.

"I wanted a little private talk." Deborah dropped her voice to a guarded murmur. "After you left, Kitty and I had a chat and we decided we needn't share a room tonight, we'd be safe in our rooms now that you were chasing some proof about Flavian."

"I'm happy to know you both believe in me," I grunted.

"We do!" Her gray-green eyes were warm. "But, after it got dark, I got to thinking I'd feel a whole lot safer with you around. Just the two of us in my room. We won't be distrubed, Kitty will be tucked up in her own little bed sleeping happily. I figured if you come to my room just before midnight, Kitty will never know the difference." She licked her bottom lip slowly. "And don't worry if you have insomnia, Danny. Like I told you before I know a marvelous cure for it, something unique!" Her hand squeezed my arm tightly for a moment. "Just before midnight, now don't forget!" Her smile was more a threat than a promise. "If you're not there on time, I'll come looking for you."

I went on into the bar and found Lenore Brophy and Eldridge already established there. They both

94

turned their heads as they heard my footsteps, then Lenore looked away pointedly. As I got close, I saw Eldridge's face was flushed and his eyes were glittering brightly. His bottom lip was still swollen from the backhander Freidel had given him earlier.

"It's a democratic bar, Mr. Boyd." His voice was slightly thick. "Everyone gets to make their own drinks."

I moved around to the back of the marble-topped bar and started making myself a rye on the rocks. Lenore looked cool in a green see-through dress, beneath which I could see her breasts in sensuous detail. Her short copper-blond hair emphasized the classic oval-shaped face and prominent cheekbones.

"I'm sure we've met," I said tentatively. "I'm Danny Boyd."

Her sapphire eyes looked at me with a frigid gaze. "We've met, Mr. Boyd. I'm the girl you left to the tender mercies of Lieutenant Schell this morning, in case you've forgotten."

"You know how it is with those police lieutenants, like they always figure three's a crowd," I said.

"I've just been hearing what a busy little Boyd you've been this afternoon. From what Flavian tells me, you managed to dig up enough motives to make the murder look like a group affair."

"You know how it is"—I felt a nasty twinge as I realized I was already repeating myself within a couple of sentences—"if you keep tossing nasty accusations around, you sometimes get some very interesting reactions."

"Flavian's a devoted fan of yours, too," she sneered. "One of your nasty accusations got him a fat lip!"

"I'll freely admit I dislike you intensely, Mr. Boyd," Eldridge volunteered. "But I hold Dion entirely responsible for what happened." He lifted his glass and drank deeply. "It's the ingratitude that hurts!"

I stared hard at Lenore until she flushed slightly, then shook my head in silent admiration. "You don't even look tired," I said in a wondering voice.

"Should I?" she snapped.

"After not even getting to bed at all last night?" I shrugged. "I'd be dead on my feet right now!"

Her face tightened. "Somehow, I can sense the usual snide approach in this. Why don't you spell it out for me, Danny?"

"You told me you went to Freidel's room just before one A.M. and he figured you were the Cathcart woman he was obviously expecting, when you knocked on the door. So then you bust into her room and fixed her wagon by telling her you were on your way to spend the night with Dion, and you were letting her know to save her any embarrassment, right?"

She nodded. "That's right, Danny. And please! Don't worry about exposing my personal life in front of Flavian. I'm sure he's lapping up every word!"

"Then you went back to your own room," I continued, "and curled up in the closet?"

"I suppose that has to mean something?"

"This morning, your bed hadn't been slept in," I said. "The Cathcart woman was expecting Dion to visit her room so your spiel didn't worry her any; not until it got real late, then she figured she'd better check your story. She went into his room and found it empty. I'm just curious to know what the both of you were doing that took all night and, if it's the obvious answer, where were you?"

"I think you've lost your mind!" Her eyes were dark with fury. "You wouldn't notice any difference, naturally. The story I told you was perfectly true, and I didn't spend the rest of the night with Dion!"

"With who, then?" I snarled.

"I'm completely fascinated by all these comings and goings through the night!" Eldridge giggled spitefully.

"Don't tell us you were with Deborah, or Kitty? I've always been so sure they were both man-girls."

"You've got a sewer of a mind, Flavian," she said bitterly. "Wherever I was in my own damned business!"

"Not when somebody murdered Stephanie last night," I growled.

"When Lieutenant Schell asks me, maybe I'll tell him. But nobody else, and least of all you, Danny!" She blinked rapidly, fighting back the tears. "You know somthing?" Her voice was unsteady. "You're about the biggest bastard I ever met in my whole life!" Then she slid off the barstool and half-ran out of the room.

The hiatus lasted long enough for me to make myself another drink. Eldridge pushed his empty glass across the bar top toward me in an exaggerated gesture.

"Fill it up, bartender!" He chuckled gleefully. "Let me drink to the greatest detective of them all!"

I pushed the glass back toward him. "Like you said, it's a democratic bar."

"You could at least pass the bottle."

"Okay, so what are you drinking?"

"I don't mind," he said petulantly, "the nearest bottle will do fine. I'm not drinking because I enjoy it, Mr. Boyd, just to get drunk."

"I can understand how you feel," I said sympathetically. "Freidel treating you the way he did, after all the work you've done on the new collection." I poured a generous couple of ounces of rye into his glass, and added a couple of ice cubes for luck before I placed the drink in front of him. "It's like you said, ingratitude!"

"It's nice to find somebody that understands," he said in a maudlin voice. "I slaved my heart out on that collection and who'll get the credit? Dion, of course!

And then he treats me like some kind of a slave. You know he hit me?"

"I was there." I nodded gravely. "It's not right, Flavian. You working night and day with Stephanie helping you, and what was Dion doing all that time?"

"She didn't do it for me, you know." His eyes were bright as sand-washed pebbles in his flushed face. "It was for Dion."

I waited until he'd taken a hefty swig from the fresh drink, then said in a very casual voice. "What happened to Dion? He just ran out of ideas?"

"Who knows, Mr. Boyd? It seemed like he just lost interest suddenly a couple of months back and"—he straightened up on the barstool and stared at me blankly for about five seconds—"oops!" He clapped his hand across his mouth, then giggled helplessly. "When I get this drunk, I don't know what I'm saying! Pay no attention to anything I've said, Mr. Boyd. The truth is, Stephanie helped me out with my routine work as Dion's assistant. Finding him the right materials, stuff like that. He's designed the whole collection and it's superb!"

"Where do you keep the duplicate key to the storeroom, Flavian?" I asked softly.

His eyes went out of focus as he tried to look at me, then he slid clumsily off the barstool and managed to catch hold of the edge of the bar top to steady himself. "It's always that last drink that sneaks up on you," he said thickly. "Excuse me, Mr. Boyd. Think I'll go to bed before it gets any rougher. Never did like boats when you get bad weather like this!" He lurched toward the door in the kind of parody a bad actor creates trying to play a drunk.

The blond house model made a swift sidestep to avoid a direct collision with him in the doorway, and watched interestedly as he staggered past her.

"My!" Kitty smiled warmly at me as she came

toward the bar. "Was that our darling little Flavian?" The smile faded from her face. "Maybe he's getting remorse over killing poor Stephanie!"

She was still wearing the black mini with the inserted panel of white lace frothing happily over the pouter-pigeon swell of her breasts. Her baby-blue eyes had an ingenuous look in them, but I already knew Kitty was ingenuous the way Lucretia Borgia was ingenuous.

"I'm so glad I've found you, Danny," she purred. "Where have you been all evening?"

"Around," I said vaguely.

"After you left my room, Deborah and I decided we'd be safe enough in our own rooms tonight, now we knew you were busy chasing evidence to put Flavian behind bars where he belongs."

"Is that right?" I said, and the sudden premonition gave me a sharp pain in the stomach.

"But now I don't feel so brave anymore." Her lower lip pouted tremulously. "I know Deborah will go straight to sleep happily, but I'm just not so insensitive as she is!" She lowered her voice to a throaty whisper. "Danny! I just had a brilliant idea; why don't you spend the night in my room? That way, I won't be scared anymore and naturally"—she tried hard to look demure—"I'll see you get your reward!"

"I—uh—" My voice faded into a dismal croak.

"You don't have to thank me, you silly boy!" Her smile was sweetly understanding; also a little rigid around the edges, too. "Around midnight will be a good time, Deborah is sure to be sound asleep by then."

I watched the rhythmic bounce of her nicely-plump bottom, given that extra something by the half-jiggle, half-shiver, that came on the offbeat, until she reached the doorway. Then she turned around and gave me a brilliant smile.

"Now don't you be late, Danny." She wagged a playful finger at me. "Or I'll—"

"I know," I said dismally. "You'll come looking for me."

After she had gone I finished my drink, went to make a fresh one, then thought better of it. With the long night stretching in front of me, I needed to stay sober. I had a choice; I could either leap out of Kitty's bed into Deborah's bed and vice versa all night, like the knucklehead hero of a B-grade European movie, or I could play tag all over the house with the both of them in determined pursuit. Why the hell was it, I wondered morosely, that when a sex fantasy turns into reality, it always becomes a nightmare?

I looked at my watch and saw it was close to a quarter after eleven already. Then—with a red-hot flash of typical Boyd brilliance—the solution hit me right between the eyes. Like all strokes of genius, the solution was magnificently simple. There was only one place I could spend the night, and protect my client's interests at the same time. I chuckled gleefully to myself at the thought of those two dizzy broads playing tag with each other around the house all night, while I was safely asleep in the storeroom. All I needed now was to get the key from Freidel.

The key—to lock the door?—my mind asked the stupid question. What the hell else? I thought irritably. A moment later another red-hot flash hit me right between the eyes, and I groaned out loud because two strokes of genius in one night will tax any guy's strength. Especially when the second stroke made the immediate future a goddamned sight harder than the first. I went back up to my room and closed the door carefully, then fit the shoulder harness under my coat with the thirty-eight holstered snugly in my left armpit. I checked in the mirror and it didn't spoil the line of the Jamaican blue, which was something. The profile looked okay, except the eyes looked kind of exhausted, and I guessed I could blame my Manhattan socialite friend for that. My first appointment was for a few minutes before midnight so if I was going to be ahead of time, it looked like Deborah was going to be the lucky girl.

I knocked gently on her door a couple of minutes later and it opened a couple of inches to allow one gray-green eye to peer through the crack. "It's you, Danny," she whispered, "come right on in."

She closed the door behind me quickly, then turned around real slow, with an expectant smile on her face. "You're early, but I take that as a compliment."

She was dressed very casually, in a pair of faded jeans and a white shirt that was unbuttoned all the way down to the waistband. Her high breasts thrust toward me beneath the shirt, which under the glow of the bedside lamp was wholly transparent. She turned away from me, and the sight of her round buttocks beneath the taut faded denim was too much for me. I slapped her bottom viciously. She let out an agonized yelp and leaped a foot straight up in the air. By the time her feet hit the floor again I had the door wide open waiting, so it was no trick to give her another vicious slap which shot her out into the hallway. Her second agonized yelp was even louder than the first—loud enough to make the door to Kitty's room open suddenly.

I caught a glimpse of startled baby-blue eyes over Deborah's shoulder, then gave her another slap. I was beginning to enjoy myself. This sort of thing was beginning to turn me on. She shot forward, and two agonized yelps mingled this time as she collided heavily with Kitty and they both fell to the floor. I stepped into the room and pulled the door shut behind me. Kitty was wearing her abbreviated black robe, which had fallen open and hiked up over her bare pink rump as she fought to disentangle herself from Deborah. Kitty finally freed herself and got as far as a crouching position with her back toward me. The temptation was irresistible. I gave the plump pink-and-white cheeks a sharp slap, and with a frantic squeal, she took off like a missile. Her head homed straight into Deborah's midriff, so the next moment they were both sprawled out on the floor again.

Kitty sat up and looked at me reproachfully. She made no move to cover herself. Her breasts had fallen free of the robe, and the sight of her lying there like that was beginning to do things to me.

"I knew there had to be a way you'd get your kicks." There was something else in her expression, a softening in her eyes.

I lit a cigarette. "Any objections?" I asked.

They managed to scramble to their feet, and stood there, tenderly rubbing their injured anatomies.

"Why did you do that?" Deborah asked in a hurt tone.

"He was being masterful," Kitty said, watching me with that soft expression in her eyes.

"He's a sadist!" Deborah's voice quivered slightly.

I was staring at Kitty's exposed breasts, heaving now after their recent exertions.

"Sure," I said easily, drawing on my cigarette. "A nice sadist."

Kitty began to move toward me, the black robe flapping away from her naked body. Involuntarily, I took a step back.

"Why don't we see just how masterful he is?" she suggested to Deborah.

"Why not?" Let's see how he really performs." Quickly, Deborah came around me to the door and stood with her back against it. She unclipped her jeans, and peeled them down over her hips. She stepped out of them, then rolled her briefs down after them. The whole operation didn't take longer than about two seconds. The shirt fell away from her breasts. The patch of red hair at the base of her stomach tapered into a wisp between her legs.

"Are you ready, Mr. Boyd?"

They were converging on me from both sides, and I debated whether I should make a run for it. But then I told myself I was being a fool. Here was an opportunity being thrown at me which mightn't come my way again for some time.

Kitty was purring from the back of her throat as she came up to me, and reaching for my belt, she began to unfasten it. I didn't resist. Nor did I resist when she eased my pants down over my hips, then my shorts. My erect log sprang free, and she took hold of it. I didn't need her help to take off my shirt, then my shoes and socks, and then to kick my pants free of my ankles. My cock throbbed in the warm cavern of Kitty's hand. Deborah pressed herself against my back and rustled her fingers through the hair around my groin. Her warm body pressed against my buttocks.

"You did it to her," Deborah said softly. "Now you can do it to me."

Their positions changed. Deborah bent forward over a chair. Her upturned buttocks shivered expectantly in front of me as I raised my hand, hesitated for a fraction, then brought it sharply down on the smooth curved flesh. She gave a short sharp cry and her body twitched forward. Kitty dropped onto her knees in front of me, her mouth closed around my hanging stem, her jaw muscles working vigorously as her hands ran up the backs of my thighs to my buttocks. I kept slapping Deborah's bottom, and an angry red mark appeared in the wake of my blows.

After a few of these slaps, Deborah decided she had had enough. She straightened, and taking my hand, pulled me free of Kitty and led me across to the bed. Both of them pushed me down on it, then while Kitty resumed her former position, Deborah straddled my head and lowered herself onto me. Her hips began to move in a gentle writhing motion. Kitty was doing clever things with her tongue and the tips of her teeth. My own tongue worked and worried the slippery flesh that folded over the lower part of my face. I was almost suffocating.

It didn't take long. Before I could do anything about it, the sensation stirred more violently, then came in one unchecked rush. My teeth bit into Deborah's crisp flesh, and with a startled yelp, she jumped away from me. I could feel my burning seed spurting into the back of Kitty's throat, but she still hung doggedly on while she drained every last drop.

A short while later, when we had all dressed again, more or less, I said, "Right. Now that the preliminaries are over, I want a few straight answers. Like why did Dion lose interest in designing?"

"We don't know. He just did." Deborah bit her lower lip pensively. Her face was still flushed. Kitty looked very pleased with herself, like the cat that's just had all the cream. "I guess it's a terrific strain the whole time. It's about the most competitive business in the whole world, and you can't afford to guess wrong. This year he started out with a half-dozen ideas, but none of them worked out right. At first he blamed Flavian for not getting the right material, then he blamed Lenore for bad cutting. For a while there he nearly drove both of them clean out of their minds. His next batch of new designs didn't work out any better. He had the lot of us slinking around the house trying to keep out of his way, because he was always screaming his head off at somebody. Then, one day, Flavian couldn't take it anymore, so he showed Dion a sketch and said that was the way it should be done. It worked out just fine, and Dion got very sarcastic and said he supposed Flavian had a whole bunch of other designs that would work out just fine."

"And he did?" I said.

She nodded slowly. "I guess that was when Dion started to lose interest. We all just sat around for a couple of weeks waiting for him to come back on the rebound. Finally, we realized it just wasn't going to happen because Dion was through. I think the thing that really destroyed him was when he knew Flavian's designs were so much better than his own. But we felt sure he'd get over it in time, and if we could all make a success of this collection in his name, he'd have the time. A wonderful guy like Dion deserves a break."

"We all love him," Kitty said in a hushed voice. "I'd give my right arm for him anytime he asked!"

"I guess Flavian loved him, too?" I said easily.

Kitty let out a nervous hiccup, then clapped her hand to her mouth, her eyes signaling frantically to Deborah.

"I knew there was something that didn't add up in the story you gave me about Stephanie finding Flavian in the storeroom, with the shears in his hand. You said she found the door unlocked, so she just walked in. If he had a duplicate key, the first thing he would have done was lock the door in back of him. So, if by any mischance Dion suddenly decided to go to the storeroom, Flavian would have some warning because he'd hear the key turn in the lock." I saw the misery grow in their eyes as they watched me with stony faces. "The only person who wouldn't bother locking the door while they were ruining the collection would be Dion, because he knew he had the only key to the storeroom, and he also knew everybody else was aware of it. Once the day's work had been put away for the night, everyone presumed the storeroom was locked until the following morning, so Dion would *know* logically that he was safe with an unlocked door in back of him."

"You see," Kitty quavered, "when the trouble first started we all thought it must be one of us doing it because they hated Flavian."

"Flavian thought the same thing," Deborah volunteered. "None of us even dreamed of suspecting Dion!"

"Until Stephanie walked in and caught him in the act?" I said.

"He didn't threaten to kill her," Kitty said quickly. "We just kind of threw that in to make you concentrate on Dion."

"How about just telling me the story the way Stephanie told it to you?" I grated.

"Dion pleaded with her not to tell anybody. He said he knew his jealousy had gotten out of hand, because his pride couldn't stand the thought that maybe Flavian was a better designer than he was. Stephanie said he made her all kinds of promises like he'd go see a psychiatrist when the showing was finished, but she still wasn't sure what she should do. I think, after all the work she'd done helping Flavian get the new collection ready on time, she found it hard to forgive him. She was also worried that he wouldn't keep his promise to stay away from the collection, and he could do something even worse to try and stop the showing. I said she should stick by Dion, like the rest of us would. If he was sick in his mind, he needed our protection more than ever! Finally, she said she'd think it over and went to her room."

"Kitty told me all about it first thing next morning," the redhead said. "I agreed with her, of course, and we went to talk to Stephanie but she wasn't in her room. Then we heard she'd been murdered during the night."

"And you figured Freidel had killed her?" I said in an awed voice. "So, instead of telling either the lieutenant or me what you knew, you decided to dangle a big phony carrot under my nose! Keep me chasing after Eldridge so I wouldn't have the time to even think about Freidel. The both of you happily decided to protect a guy you already knew was psychotic—sabotaging the new collection proved that!—and you fully believed was a murderer?"

"Well," Deborah said uncertainly, "I'll admit it does sound funny the way you put it, but you just don't know Dion the way we do."

"For sure, you don't love him the way we do!" Kitty said in an accusing voice. "How do you know Dion did kill Stephanie, anyway?"

"I don't," I whimpered. "The whole goddamned point is that, even after you were both convinced in your own minds that Dion had killed Stephanie, you were still determined to protect . . ." My voice died on me right then, as I began to feel the impact of their implacable hostility.

Deborah gave me a bright, patently false smile. "So what are you going to do now, Danny?"

The silence seemed to crowd into the room while I thought up an answer. They were both completely still, hardly breathing, their eyes fixed unblinkingly on my face. I had a sudden sure conviction that one wrong answer from me, and their tails wouldn't even rattle before they struck.

"Well." I forced a grin onto my face. "I guess I can't blame you for feeling the way you do about Dion. There's nothing more I can do tonight, anyway. It seems a shame I can't hang around a little longer."

"Why not?" Kitty said slinkily. "There's a hell of a lot more we can show you. That was only an appetizer—right, Deborah?"

Deborah winked lewdly at me. "Right, Kitty."

I looked at them, interested. "Well, maybe . . ." I demurred.

"The three of us can have a real ball," Deborah opined.

"A real ball," Kitty repeated. "After we've had a shower and a couple of minutes to plan our campaign. Come on, Deborah."

The moment the door shut, I moved across to the bureau and went through the drawers like a maniac, tossing anything that looked useful onto the bed. By the time I had finished there was a small pile of loot making a pyramid on the bedcover. The bathroom door opened a minute later and I heard the shower running for a brief moment until the door closed again.

"Debbie has this fetish thing about taking a shower last thing before she goes to bed," Kitty explained sweetly. "It doesn't matter if she's already had four showers during the day she"—her eyes goggled as she saw the loot on the bed—"what are they doing there?"

"I'll explain," I said gently, then put my arm around her shoulders and walked her over to the bed. "Close your eyes for a moment!"

"All right." She closed her eyes obediently but her voice sounded dubious. "I hope you're not one of those kinky characters, Danny?"

I eased the thirty-eight out of the harness, pressed the barrel against her forehead and clamped my other hand over her mouth at the same time. "One squeak out of you," I whispered, "and I'll blow the top of your head clean off!" Her eyeballs jiggled frantically, but she managed to nod her head.

I took my hand away from her mouth and she got the shakes. After I had pulled the covers back I made her lie face down on the bed, then made a quick selection from the loot I had taken from her bureau. A pair of briefs made an effective gag secured by a cloth belt knotted at the nape of her neck. I tied her arms to her sides with the legs of a pair of jeans, and used another pair for her ankles, then pulled the covers up again until only the top of her blonde head showed above them.

Deborah emerged from the bathroom a little later, all naked and gleaming. She gaped when she saw the top of Kitty's head above the covers, then gurgled with laughter.

"Don't tell me the poor kid's beat. Well, well, well." She shook her head in consideration.

I laughed along with her as I pulled out the thirty-eight again and made her lie face-down on the bed alongside her chum. There was enough loot left to fix her up more or less the same way as Kitty. I removed the key from the inside of the door and took a last look at them before I locked them in for the night.

"It would have been a ball," I said regretfully. "It was—what there was of it. So why did the both of you have to go and get yourselves tied up at the last moment?"

The moment before I switched off the light, I saw the covers writhe in a kind of impotent frenzy.

Chapter NINE

I went down one flight of the circular staircase and found the bar was deserted. If Lenore had been in her room, I figured all that hollering as I spanked Deborah across the hallway would have brought her out real fast to see who was being murdered. So I went down the second flight of stairs and found the dining room was empty. The workrooms were worth a try, before I started disturbing the other guests in their rooms.

The door to Freidel's workroom was half-open and the lights were on. As I walked into the room I saw he was in his favorite place, perched on the edge of his workbench, an unlit panatela clenched between the fingers of his right hand. Lenore was sitting slumped forward in one of the straight-backed chairs, her elbows on her knees and her face buried in her hands. My footsteps sounded loud in the still room but neither of them bothered to look up. I stopped beside Lenore's chair and put my hand on her shoulder.

"I know about Dion running out of ideas," I said softly. "How the rest of you made a conspiracy to keep it a secret from his partners. You cut from Flavian's designs, and the house models helped out, especially Stephanie. Dion tried to ruin the collection because it wasn't his at all, and he couldn't accept the fact that he'd been out-designed by his own assistant. Stephanie walked into the storeroom to try and return that dress and caught him at it. So now there's no reason why you can't tell me where you were all of last night."

She lifted her head slowly and looked at me with empty eyes. I saw how the skin was drawn tight across the bones of her face and colored with a dirty gray pallor.

"It's too late now," she said in a dull monotone. "What happened last night isn't important anymore."

"I'd like to hear it all the same."

Her copper-blond head nodded listlessly. "If it amuses you, Danny. I told you the truth before, as far as it went. When I found you weren't in your room I got mad at you, then I decided I'd see if I got a better reception from Dion. He asked me into his room and I could see by the look on his face that something dreadful had happened. He told me how he'd been deliberately sabotaging the new collection and how Stephanie had caught him at it earlier in the night. Most of the time he talked, he was crying, and obviously suffering from a deep emotional disturbance. After a while he mentioned his date with the Cathcart woman, how she was waiting for him in the room next door. He was obviously in no condition to keep the date, so I walked into her room like I told you before and fixed that one! Then I went along to Stephanie's room, hoping to convince her she shouldn't tell anyone what she'd found out, but she wasn't there. I ran back to Dion's room, told him Stephanie was missing and we'd better find her quickly before she blew the whole situation. So we both went looking for her."

"It was during that time Libby Cathcart walked into his room and found it empty, I guess?" I said.

"It must have been."

"You went looking for Stephanie?" I prompted her.

"We searched all through the house without finding her, then went out into the grounds"—I felt the smooth flesh of her shoulders tremble under my hand—"and we found her when we reached the pool. Dion nearly went out of his mind. He blamed himself for her death, and kept on saying it would never have happened if he hadn't allowed himself to be consumed by jealousy. I finally managed to quieten him down and we came back inside the house. I spent the rest of the night with him in his room. He needed someone to comfort him, to hold him close in the dark. How could I leave him alone with all his nightmares, and now this dreadful feeling of guilt?"

"And went back to your own room in the morning?"

"Yes." She gave me the same listless nod of her head. "But before I left I told him if anybody should ask, to say he had spent the night with Libby. He wasn't in a fit state to realize he would automatically be the main suspect, if Stephanie had talked to anyone before she was murdered."

There was a faint rustling sound as the panatela snapped between Freidel's fingers. "It's all done," he said, his voice a whispering echo of the former vigorous bass. "Finished! Who will cry for the lost talent of Dion Freidel when he's buried under an avalanche of filthy publicity?"

"Not me," I snarled, "I could wish it had happened sooner, then maybe Stephanie would still be alive."

"Don't be cruel, Danny," Lenore said in the same dull monotone. "You're talking to a dead man, as far as any future for him is concerned."

"Since when did this happen?" I snapped.

"Since Flavian walked in here about an hour back, blind malicious drunk."

"A man's sins keep pace with him even if he doesn't hear them," Freidel whispered. "The man you are beholden to is the one who will destroy you in the end."

"You need something to keep you occupied," I told him. "Why don't you shove another cigar in your mouth, then set fire to your moustache?"

"You can't stop him now, Danny," Lenore said. "He's finally equated with his guilt, and he's just beginning to enjoy it."

"Okay," I said sourly. "So what happened when the loaded Flavian staggered in here?"

"We were in the middle of a meeting to finalize some of the details for the showing. Harry Kempton, Luman, and Reilly were here. Dion asked me along ostensibly to fill in some of the facts, but he really wanted me around as a kind of emotional crutch. The door was closed and we were in the middle of some dull piddling little organization problem, when Flavian arrived. He nearly slammed the door right off its hinges when he came into the room. I took one look at him and knew the sky was about to come crashing down on our heads. Everyone stopped talking, naturally, and they all watched him lurch across the room toward Dion. He demanded the key to the storeroom, then Luman told him he was drunk and to get the hell out. Flavian turned around and snapped his fingers under Art's nose—or tried to, anyway—then told him little fat men never could understand why first things were first in order of their importance."

"I'd like to have seen Luman's face right then," I sighed.

"I thought there'd be a loud bang and he'd fly apart in small pieces. He was about to hit Flavian, I'm sure of it, but Reilly grabbed his arm, then asked Flavian in a real polite voice just what was of first importance?"

"And the son of a bitch told him!" Freidel whispered. " 'To make sure *my* collection is protected against any further maniacal attacks,' he said. Then he rambled on about how, in his considered opinion the man we'd hired—that's you, Boyd—was only an amateur incompetent. I gave him the key right then, hoping it would shut him up. But it was already too late."

"Harry was too upset by the disturbance to listen properly to what Flavian was saying," Lenore said wearily. "Luman was still sputtering mad at him and I thought for a moment we'd gotten away with it, but Chuck Reilly had absorbed every word. He started flattering Flavian's drunken ego by saying how much he appreciated the rightness of his putting first things first. For sure, there was nothing more important than protecting the new collection against malicious damage. Then he slid the knife into Flavian right up to the hilt!"

"It was neat," Freidel whispered with a kind of gloomy admiration in his voice. "He had Flavian almost wagging his tail gratefully for all the compliments he was giving him. Then he casually tossed in the grenade. He valued Flavian's opinion, he said solemnly, so he hoped Flavian agreed with him that this new collection showed a dazzling brilliance in original designs that had never been formerly achieved. And while Flavian was about to float up to the ceiling in ecstasy, Reilly said it was beyond doubt that with this new collection, Dion Freidel had surpassed himself."

"The gernade exploded right there," Lenore said flatly. "Flavian ranted and screamed and almost tore out his own hair. Reilly just sat back in his chair with a nasty grin on his face and listened while Flavian spilled the whole story!"

"I feel sorry for Harry, in a remote kind of way," Freidel announced generously. "There won't be any showing now, of course. So the company will inevitably lose money over the current financial year. Luman will buy out Harry cheap, but at least he'll get something back. All I've gotten so far is the threat of certain exposure to the whole goddamned world, and the promise of a raft of lawsuits which will add up to around five million dollars, approximately."

"Don't forget the punch on the nose from Art Luman, Dion," Lenore added, and I hoped I heard a faint degree of satisfaction in her voice.

"That clumsy fat oaf couldn't hurt a fag like Flavian, even," Freidel said with great dignity. "He was lucky I didn't kill him!"

"And Chuck Reilly wouldn't have been a factor in your decision?" I asked politely.

He brushed his moustache vigorously with his index finger, then folded his arms across his chest and stared impassively into space. "The greatest sin was pride," he whispered after what seemed a long silence. "But I have the rest of my life to atone. The more my enemies mock and scourge me, the more I will bend my head and the greater will my atonement be."

"If things get real tough, you can always rent him out for Halloween parties," I said to Lenore in a loud voice.

"Please stop it," she said fiercely. "He's suffering enough already."

"Ah, come on!" I exploded. "He's still the same fourteen-carat phony he always was, only more so, if that's possible. Let him get away with this crap and he'll wind up making a tape out of it, then sit around and listen to himself for the rest of his lousy life!"

She lifted her head quickly and glared at me. I felt that almost tangible hostility emanating from her, and once again, wherever Freidel and his women were involved, I was swamped by a feeling of complete futility.

"You just don't understand him, Danny." Her voice was laced with a sneering contempt. "He's such an incomparably greater man—even right now at this very moment!—than you can hope to be, it makes you secretly envy him, doesn't it? You're no different from the others; Kempton, Luman, Reilly, Flavian! You all feel you have to keep trying to pull him down into your miserable little gutters the whole time! But we won't let you do it."

"We?" I gurgled.

"Those of us who love him," she said proudly.

"We'll always protect him from the envy and malice of the mean little men like you."

"If you keep on, honey," I said mildly, "Dion will get mad at you for not letting him get a word in edgewise." I grinned at her and it froze right there on my face when I saw ferocious hatred lurking in the back of her eyes. "Just one question," I pleaded. "After the grenade exploded and the sky fell in, what happened to our friend Flavian?"

"I have no idea." Lenore leaned her head back and closed her eyes deliberately. "It's my sincere hope that he sobered up enough to realize exactly what he'd done, then killed himself!"

"I seem to remember," Freidel whispered, "he wandered out of the room while my former partners and I were busy screaming at each other. As he had the key clutched in his clammy little hand, I imagine you'll find him in the storeroom. Still swooning in ecstasy, I don't doubt, as he savors the unsurpassed brilliance of his own creations!"

I took the precaution of moving away from Lenore's chair before I said respectfully, "I guess you'd know how he feels, Dion. I mean, what with your have been a fashion designer yourself at one time, and all."

A faint hissing sound from the direction of Lenore's chair pursued me as I walked quickly to the door. I climbed the circular staircase back to the top floor, then walked down the hallway to the storeroom. The door was closed, but when I turned the doorknob gently it opened a half-inch. A nervous itch around the short hairs at the nape of my neck rapidly became insistent. It was the kind of primitive intuition that made me yank out the thirty-eight fast. I flattened myself against the wall, reached out with one foot and prodded the door open another six inches.

"Flavian?" I said softly. "Are you in there?"

All I heard in reply was the pulse-beat inside my

own eardrums. I waited maybe another ten seconds, then lashed out with my foot so the door rocketed back onto its hinges. There was still no reaction so I pulled down the shades on the thinking part of my mind and went into the storeroom fast—in a kind of gorilla crouch—and found it was empty. I straightened up, took a long deep breath, and holstered the gun. The door to the closet stood wide open and I could see the hanger parade of the collection that never would be shown now, stacked tight together along the rails. They looked wrong, somehow. I moved in for a closer look and saw the floor of the closet was littered with odd-shaped pieces of material. Then I was close enough to see that someone had taken a sharp knife to the whole collection; hacked and slashed away until they were sure every single garment was effectively destroyed.

The mute evidence of unrestrained violence gave me an uneasy feeling deep in the pit of my stomach. I moved away from the closet and noticed a neat pile of clothing in back of the ancient couch. When I bent down for a closer look, that uneasy feeling in my stomach developed into a sharp stabbing pain. There was a coat, pants, shirt, tie, socks, and shoes, and they all belonged to Eldridge. I recognized them as the clothes he had been wearing in the bar earlier, and, in any case, the kind of clothes he favored were very distinctive—like only one man in every million would have the gall to be seen dead in them.

So why should Flavian have a sudden compulsion to prance around in his jockey shorts? The slashed remnants of what had been his magnificent achievement up until an hour back were painfully visible from where I was standing. I started to put them together with the neat pile of his clothes in back of the couch, and wished I hadn't when I kept coming up with the same answer the whole time. A few seconds later I moved slowly over to the window—and looked down into darkness. The sharp stabbing pain leaped out of the pit of my stomach and started stabbing all over.

I came pounding back into the workroom like the cavalry to the rescue—and, like them, probably too late already—skidded to a stop, then had to wait to catch my breath. Friedel and Lenore watched me with a mild curiosity showing on their faces until I had enough breath to speak.

"The pool lights," I said to Freidel. "Where's the switch?"

"Why," he blinked slowly. "Is there something wrong?"

"They're out," I gasped. "My guess is somebody switched them off for a good reason, like to hide the fact there's another body floating in the pool."

"Whose?" Lenore whispered.

"Flavian's, maybe." I glared at Freidel. "Are you going to put them on again or just sit there like a wooden Indian, full of termite holes!"

"I'm coming," he muttered, and slid off the workbench onto his feet.

"I'll come with you," Lenore said determinedly.

"Make it a party if you want," I growled. "Just so we get those lights back on again."

The master switch was in the basement, Freidel explained as we headed toward the front door, and he'd better check that out first. Outside, there was enough starlight to find our way across the grass, and we had nearly reached the pool when the lights came on. The twin circles glowed with subdued light, the diving-board complex preened and glittered with floodlit pride, and even the drink-wagon lit up as the lamp fixed to the underside of its orange-colored umbrella shone again. We came onto the concrete surround and stood beside the drink-wagon until our eyes adjusted to the light.

"I don't see any—" That was about as far as Lenore

got before she let out a piercing scream that jangled my nerve ends together like a bunch of broken glass beads. "Danny!" Her voice was some kind of a gargle deep in her throat, while her fingers gouged into my arm. "Don't you see it? Over there, right on the edge!"

I followed the line of her pointing finger, which was obviously suffering from an acute palsy, then finally saw *something* lying there at the edge.

"It's not big enough for a body," I told her.

"I know it is!" She tried to stop her teeth from chattering, then gave me a sudden violent shove in the small of the back. "Go find out!" she snapped. "If I don't die of fright first, I'll die from not knowing!"

There was the sickening realization that Lenore had been right, when I got close enough to see the slim bare legs, the tops of the thighs just covered by the hem of a dress. What had fooled me at a distance was that the body was half-in and half-out of the pool. The head was under the water, the top half of the torso spanned the distance between the edge of the pool and the surface of the water, while the bottom half, from the waist to the feet, was sprawled out on the concrete.

"Oh, my God!" Lenore's voice whimpered directly in back of me. "It's a woman!"

I kneeled down at the edge and was abruptly conscious that in the immediate vicinity of the head there was an area of water darker and more vicious-looking than the water in the rest of the pool. I straddled the lower half of the body, slid my hands forward under its chest and carefully inched it backward until the whole body lay face-down on the concrete.

"The poor kid!" a muted bass said someplace close.

I looked up and saw Freidel standing about four feet away from me, one arm wrapped protectively around Lenore's shoulders. She had her face buried in his chest and was sobbing quietly.

"Who was she?" Freidel asked in a cracked voice.

"You ask the damndest questions!" I said thinly. "Take a good look at her legs."

He shuffled closer, bringing Lenore with him, then leaned his head forward as he stared down at the thin white legs. "Boyd?" His voice was so faint I almost didn't hear him. "The legs? They're all wrong!"

"Too skinny, too much hard muscle, and way too hairy," I grunted.

"I don't understand." Panic started to edge into his voice. "The dress, and all! Who—"

I pushed my hands under the shoulders and slowly rolled the body onto its back. The head and neck dragged behind the rest of the body as it turned, as if they were reluctant to be exposed. Then, at the last moment, the head rolled in a tight arc and the face was staring directly at me. I closed my eyes tight for maybe five seconds, then opened them again. Flavian Eldridge still stared straight at me with a wide grin splitting his face. Only it wasn't a grin, I realized as I climbed slowly back onto my feet, it was the gaping wound in his neck where his throat had been cut, almost from ear to ear.

The few yards to the drink-wagon seemed a hell of a long way. I grabbed hold of the nearest bottle, unscrewed the stopper, then tilted it to my lips. My taste buds didn't function so I had no idea what I was drinking but when I finally stopped, the level had lowered around four inches and there was a faint warmth right at the bottom of the cavern where my stomach used to be. I lit a cigarette very carefully, and the match didn't waver that much.

In back of me, Lenore's muted sobbing was suddenly drowned out by the harsher sound of Freidel retching violently.

Chapter TEN

Lenore sat motionless in an armchair, her eyes half-closed, and her face looked haggard under the light. Freidel was playing bartender in back of the marble-topped bar, making himself two drinks for every one he served. Perched on a barstool, with his haunches overflowing in every which way, Luman looked like some revolting carrion crow. Beside him, Reilly was leaning against the bar in an apparently relaxed stance, but you could see the computers clicking away as his eyes continually swiveled from face to face around the room. Harry Kempton was sitting on the very edge of his armchair, his hands pressed tight together palm-to-palm and pinned between his knees. The anxious look on his face said he was scared he was about to remember something unpleasant any moment now, like a second corpse had been pulled out of the pool with its throat cut, and when he did remember, he would pass out cold. I was leaning against the wall, carefully holding my drink in my left hand, waiting to see who was going to jump first.

"We don't have much time before the police get here," Luman barked suddenly. "And we've got to do some pretty fast thinking and decision-making before they arrive. It'll be too goddamned late when they're here!" He scowled at everybody in turn. "Where are the rest of them?"

"Kitty and Deborah have been asleep for the last couple of hours," I said, not too quickly. "You don't need them, Art. What's good for Dion, they figure is good for them."

"Okay," he nodded briefly.

Kempton cleared his throat on a high-pitched note. "I suggest we—uh—hardly need either Miss Peridot or Miss Cathcart?"

"You out of your mind?" Luman roared at him. "We need them like a hole in the head."

"Who would need a hole in the head?" Kempton looked bewildered for a moment, then his face brightened. "Ah! I see the point. Nobody *needs* a hole in the head!"

Luman turned toward Reilly with a disgusted look on his face. "Out of all the guys in the world—in California, even!—you could make a partnership deal with, we had to go and pick him!"

"Let's get to the decision-making, Art," Freidel said. I wondered if the liquor had brought his voice back to its normal resonant bass, or if it was something else again?

"Yeah." Luman glared around the room again. "First thing, we've got to get our story straight about Eldridge. That's vital!" He picked up his drink from the bar top. "You tell 'em, Chuck."

"It's simple," Reilly said in an easy voice. "We just tell the police the truth. In the beginning Dion was generous enough to allow Eldridge to design a handful of originals for the new collection. Nobody realized what effect this would have on his paranoiac ego. As time went on, he convinced himself his designs were far superior to those of Dion's, and somehow he was being cheated. But he was cunning, too. He knew if the collection was a failure, Art could buy out both his partners in the company." He nodded toward me. "That theory of yours was fifty percent right, Boyd. When Eldridge started in to ruin the collection it wasn't just for personal revenge—to even the score with Dion—he was also hoping that when the collection failed and Dion was no longer a partner, he'd take over as the designer."

"How about Stephanie?" I asked.

"That poor girl!" He shook his head slowly. "She forgot to return one of the new dresses in time for it to be locked away, so she raced up to the storeroom, hoping she'd catch Dion before he'd locked it for the night, then found the door wasn't locked. So she walked right in on Eldridge busy ruining some more dresses! He begged her not to tell Dion, then threatened to kill her if she did. Stephanie was so scared she told him she'd think it over and let him know her decision in the morning. Only he came to his own decision that he couldn't trust her long before morning!"

"So he killed her?" I said.

"That's right," Reilly nodded. "Tonight, after all that drunken boasting in Dion's workroom, he must have realized he'd condemned himself out of his own mouth. No paranoiac could accept a failure like that. So he took a knife with him to the storeroom and methodically slashed every garment in the whole collection until it was completely ruined—except one. His personal favorite out of his own designs." He grimaced sharply. "We all know what Eldridge was, and maybe that's why he put on that dress. A last sneer at the rest of us, flaunting his difference even in death. Who knows? Then he pulled the master switch so all the pool lights went out, took the knife with him to the edge of the pool, knelt down on the concrete and"—he shrugged—"that was it."

There was a short silence then Freidel said, "Art?"

"What is it?" Luman snarled.

"I think I can remember all the details about Flavian okay, but I'll be honest with you and come right out with it, Art! Flavian's dead, the rest of us are alive, and the company's immediate future interests me a hell of a lot more right now than Flavian's motives for doing what he did."

"I must say," Kempton chimed in eagerly, "I'm in complete agreement with Dion. As he says, what of the immediate future?"

"It's easy." Safe in their deep rolls of fat, Luman's piggy eyes glittered expectantly. "You don't have a new collection—Eldridge saw to that!—so you don't have a showing. That means you do get a loss this financial year. So then I buy the both of you out real cheap, and I guess you get into some other line of work!"

"But that's outrageous!" Kempton's voice strengthened with his own anger. "You know what's been happening here, Art! You know why we don't have a new collection anymore! To take advantage of us both in this way is highway robbery!"

"Art?" Freidel brushed his moustache carefully for a moment. "I find I've got a problem here. Suddenly I can't remember any details of the story Chuck told us. I know he said it was important we should all remember it, but—"

"You don't have any problems, Dion," Luman chuckled. "Right after I buy you out as a partner, I make you a deal. Come straight back in as the designer and I'll carry the overhead of this place until you're ready for the next showing, pay you a top salary plus twenty-five percent of the profit!"

"You're right, Art, I don't have any problem at all," Freidel said, as the smirk spread slowly across his face.

"You never did, Dion." Luman's beefy index finger stabbed the air as he pointed toward Kempton. "He was the only target! I can take over his end tomorrow and run it a hell of a lot more efficiently than he ever would in a thousand years! But he had that goddamned partnership deal going for him as long as the company showed a profit each year. This year they don't, so"—

he drew his finger sharply across his throat—"this year it's like good-bye to our old buddy Harry!"

"Hey, Art!" I said loudly. "If I go along with this crazy story you had Reilly feed us, what's in it for me?"

"That wasn't a crazy story, Boyd," he said in a curiously mild voice. "Chuck just laid out the simple truth for you."

"I think you're both getting confused," Reilly said smoothly. "What Boyd is really asking—and he's got every right—is what compensation does he get for all the work he's done since he's been here. I would suggest," his pause was fractional, "you should double his original fee, Art. How does that sound to you, Boyd?"

"Well, I don't think I could buy the story for four thousand bucks, Chuck," I said politely. "You don't mind me calling you Chuck?" He shook his head briefly. "But it's a real pleasure to hear the ventriloquist talking for himself. I get so tired of listening to that overweight dummy of yours run off at the mouth the whole time!"

"You—what?" Luman's neck was suddenly choked with corded veins, as his face turned a rich plum color.

"Shut up, dummy!" I said coldly. "I'm talking with your boss right now."

"Have you flipped, or something, Boyd?" Reilly asked in a thin voice.

"You remember, Mr. Kempton?" I said, keeping my eyes fixed on Reilly's face. "You told me you tried to dig up some background on Art Luman in L.A. and you couldn't find a thing? Lieutenant Schell ran the same check through the L.A. police department, only he asked for a check on Reilly at the same time."

So I was lying a little. Sometimes if you can get the guy to believe a lie, it works better than the truth. Out of the corner of my eye, I saw Freidel was listening just as hard as Kempton.

"Schell called me just before seven tonight." That bit was true, anyway. "L.A. had gotten back to him with their checks. Art Luman is a nothing, they said; a penny-ante wheeler and dealer who just doesn't rate. But, Reilly?" I shook my head slowly. "Now there's a fascinating record!"

"What are you getting at, exactly, Boyd?" Freidel asked in a worried voice.

"It's a lot more simple than Chuck's phony story about Flavian," I told him. "If you're in the business of being a bastard—and have a record to prove it!— what's an easy way out in new territory like Santo Bahia? You pick up some penny-ante bum like Luman, and pretend he's the boss, the big-shot. But you've got to be sure he does things the way you want them done, so you make yourself his associate. The guy who's always around the whole time but never says too much."

I looked at Freidel's bug-eyed expression and laughed. "You've been suckered all the way down the line, Dion! You and Kempton both! You don't seriously believe Flavian killed Stephanie, but he's dead and if he gets the blame now, you figure it'll take you off the hook as the potential prime suspect! You want to know who killed Stephanie? Chuck killed her. Flavian never killed himself, either. You remember when you smacked him in the mouth and his lip bled a little? He almost fainted in terror when he saw around three drops of his own blood. You seriously think, after the way he reacted to a cut lip, he'd walk out there in the darkness, kneel down on the edge of the pool, then use a knife to slit his own throat from ear to ear?"

"Mr. Boyd." Kempton's voice was cold and precise. "If, as I understand it, you're accusing Chuck of having committed two murders, he must have had a powerful motivation."

"Money, Mr. Kempton," I said. "To gain complete control of the company by getting rid of you and Dion.

He didn't know that Dion had run out of ideas and let Flavian design about all of the new collection, anymore than he knew it was Dion himself who was out to ruin the collection because of his own vanity. But the sabotage suited him just fine. He didn't like you hiring me, either, so he and Art between them tried to scare me into quitting. Stephanie walked in on Dion in the storeroom and caught him with a pair of shears in his hand. Dion didn't threaten, he pleaded with her not to destroy the faith of the others. What did she say to that, Dion?"

"She needed time to think it over," he mumbled, "maybe she needed advice, she said. Either way, she'd tell me her decision in the morning."

"I wonder who she'd go to for advice?" The question was strictly rhetorical because I wasn't about to let Reilly get a word in edgewise right then. "She knew the rest of the staff, including Flavian, was fanatically loyal to Dion. That would leave one of the other two partners. Did she come to you, Mr. Kempton?"

"Indeed she didn't." His voice softened for a moment. "I wish she had."

"So she went to Art Luman, and he said he'd think it over and they could make plans in the morning. That gave him time enough to tell his boss the whole story. Chuck must have figured it was Christmas when he heard the story. One of the partners he wants to unload not only didn't design the collection going out under his name but is busy trying to wreck the collection his assistant designed out of loyalty to him. Everybody is working for Chuck, even if they don't know it! But when he gets around to thinking a little more about it, he realized there was one person who wasn't working for him at all, and that was Stephanie. If the true story about Freidel ever got out it wouldn't just ruin this year's collection—which he wanted, anyway—but it would ruin the reputation of the Freidel label forever, and leave him owning a hundred percent of nothing! The story didn't have to travel far to leak, either. Right here in the house were two important Freidel clients, Libby Cathcart and Polly Peridot. If one of them even got a whisper of the truth, that would be it."

"So he coldbloodedly decided to murder the girl?" Kempton asked in a wondering voice.

"You have to understand a guy like Chuck Reilly, Mr. Kempton," I said. "There's only one rule and that is he wins. Everything else is only a calculated business risk, and the only question is will it pay off? When he decided it was necessary to murder Stephanie, the rest would have been easy. My guess is he went to her room in the early hours of the morning when he felt almost sure everyone else would be sleeping, then said Luman figured he had a solution that wouldn't hurt Dion, but he wanted to be sure they talked in secret, so he was waiting for her out by the pool. She would have slipped on the nearest available dress which happened to be of the new collection—the one that caused all the trouble in the first place. On their way out of the house, he went into Lenore's workroom and grabbed the shears off her workbench. A big guy like Chuck wouldn't have a problem in holding the girl still for long enough to cut her throat, especially when she trusted him completely up until the very last moment."

"You talk about Art running off at the mouth!" Reilly sneered. "You never stop, Boyd! You know what it sounded like to me? Another one of those goddamned theories you keep coming up with! You know, like the time you got Harry to herd us into Dion's workroom and by the time you'd finished, we were all murderers about three times over! There was just one thing wrong with all those theories, as I remember? You didn't have one single shred of proof to back up any of them!" He waited a couple of seconds to build impact for his punch line. "Is this one any different, Boyd?"

"I don't need to prove this one, Chuck." I grinned derisively at him. "You've already done that for me."

"Okay." He shrugged his shoulders impatiently. "So maybe I'm the one who's crazy. Just tell me how I did it, huh?"

"Stephanie went to one of the other girls first, before she went to Art for some advice," I said. "Kitty scolded her for not being a hundred percent loyal to Dion, and told her to keep her mouth shut. First thing in the morning, Kitty told her friend Deborah the full story. The next thing was they heard Stephanie had been murdered. There was only one obvious answer to that from their point of view; Dion must have killed her. Even then, they were still loyal to him. So they called me into their room and told me the story, but they pulled one big switch. Instead of Dion, they said it was Flavian Stephanie had found in the storeroom. They had me going for a while, too! It was only a couple of hours back I forced them to admit the truth, then I left them tied and gagged in Kitty's room, with the door locked on the outside. I've still got the key in my pocket."

"I've heard enough crap from this maniac!" Luman roared at the top of his voice. "Let's—"

"Shut up"—Kempton's voice overpowered Luman's roar—"dummy!"

Art left his mouth hanging open long enough for me to get back in. "We all heard you tell the story we should learn parrot-wise before the police get here," I said to Reilly. "By a funny coincidence, you substituted Flavian's name for Dion, although you already knew it had to be Dion after Flavian gave his drunken performance as the great designer tonight. There's a second coincidence, Chuck. Your story matches the one I heard from Kitty in every detail."

"So?" He was still alert and watchful, but only a little tense, I figured.

"If you'd heard the story from Kitty she would have told it the same as she told it to me, using Flavian's name, to protect Dion. Then you wouldn't have had any reason to kill Stephanie. If outside people, even important clients, heard the story it wouldn't matter. Some minor employee—an assistant to the great Freidel—had gone off his trolley and had been a nuisance for a while until they caught up with him. So you didn't hear it from Kitty, friend!"

"Mr. Boyd has a good argument there," Kempton snapped. "The girl went to one of her staff friends for advice and was told to stay loyal to Dion. There was no point in asking any other members of the staff because she knew they were all loyal, and they'd give her the same answer."

"So that left her with a choice of going to one of Dion's other two partners, Chuck," I said gently. "Either Kempton or Luman. You want to ask Mr. Kempton if she went to him?"

"No," he said after a long pause. "I guess I won't bother."

"The police should be here at any moment!" Kempton said gruffly.

"You think Reilly would have let Art call them until he was sure he'd sold all of us the story of Flavian Eldridge, murderer and suicide?" I said. "You have a trusting nature, Mr. Kempton?"

Reilly ran one hand slowly through his flaming thatch of hair, then grinned at me. "You're not as stupid as I figured, Boyd."

"You're every bit as dangerous as I figured, Chuck," I said sincerely.

"Mr. Kempton?" I kept my total concentration on Reilly. "I think now would be a good time for you to walk out of this room and call the police."

"Of course!"

I didn't see him get up from his chair but Luman's reaction was more than enough. The sweat was already streaming down his face and I saw the switch in his eyes the moment before he shouted, "Nobody leaves this room if they want to stay alive!"

The moment I saw his hand start to claw inside his coat, I let my knees go limp so I slid down the wall into a sitting position and yanked the thirty-eight clear of the harness at the same time. By the time the seat of my pants hit the floor, I saw Reilly had stepped behind Luman's barstool and was using his vast bulk as a shield. The gun in Art's hand joggled up and down frantically, as the spasms of stark terror shook his whole gross body.

"If I've got to shoot through you, Art," I said truthfully, "I will. You want to talk to your partner about that?"

"Shoot the stupid bastard!" Reilly's voice yelled angrily. "You needed a diversion to give you time to get your gun clear, and you pulled about the oldest gag in the world!" His voice was thick with fury. "Bring another guy into the play and catch them off-balance. And this dumb elephant fell for that 'Go call the cops, Kempton' routine! Do me a favor, Boyd; put a couple of slugs where Art's guts should be!"

While he was talking I had been edging crabwise along the wall and made around three feet. In perfect synchronization with his last word, a gun barrel suddenly appeared over Luman's right shoulder. The slug chewed plaster out of the wall about where my head would have been if I'd stayed in the same place, and I heard the angry whine of the ricochet.

"Good-bye, Art Luman!" I said, and elevated the barrel of the thirty-eight an inch so it was pointing directly at his massive stomach.

"No!" The word was a scream wrenched from the

seat of terror someplace deep inside him. At the same moment he lunged forward in a frantic effort to get off the barstool, but his legs were too short and his weight at least eighty pounds too heavy. It was like watching a one-reel silent comedy that went back to the days before Mack Sennett. Luman still held his head and shoulders hunched forward, his eyes riveted on his ultimate goal—the floor—while every ounce of fat in his body writhed and quaked in a gigantic effort to achieve the impossible: to lift his vast bulk a couple of inches into the air before his feet had touched the floor.

I heard Reilly's jeering cackle of laughter, then Dion suddenly came to life. Up until then he'd been standing behind the bar like he'd been turned into an iceberg the moment the gunplay had started. Maybe it was Reilly's rasping laugh that did it. The hell with reasons, I thought, just keep the action going! His right hand suddenly shot forward, grabbed the neck of the nearest bottle, swung it high in the air, then slammed it down across the back of Luman's head. It was just the momentum Art had been looking for, even if he didn't appreciate it at the time it was applied.

The bottle made a nasty wet kind of sound on impact, and didn't break. For an awe-inspiring moment, Luman's body teetered on the point of no return, then he and the barstool crashed onto the floor with a sound like an earthquake had hit.

The moment Luman teetered, I lined up the thirty-eight on a point a couple of inches below his left shoulder and held it there. When he passed the point of no return, the shoulder moved slowly at first, revealing another shoulder in back of it. His crash to the floor was a brief cataclysmic affair, like one moment I was watching a shoulder in back of his, and the next moment I could see all of Chuck Reilly, right down to the startled look on his face. I squeezed the trigger carefully three times and the sound of the shots were a minor encore to the magnificent explosive sound Art's body had made when it met the floor. Maybe the first slug parted his hair, or more probably missed him altogether. The second slug parted his teeth, and I lost interest in the third because it wasn't important anymore.

Lenore managed to get halfway out of her chair, then looked at Reilly's body and fainted straight back into it again. Kempton went to make his delayed call to the cops, and I went down on my knees to take a close look at Art Luman.

"He's still alive," I said when I got back onto my feet. "I'd figure you fractured his skull with that bottle, for sure."

"It was nothing!" Dion smiled proudly. "But saving the lives of everyone present in this room tonight has assuaged some of my guilt. I know I shall start designing again very soon now."

Kempton came back with a worried look on his face and said Schell had promised to be out to the house within the next ten minutes."

"Fine," I said.

"He was very strange on the phone," Kempton confided in a puzzled voice. "He asked me if you'd killed anybody and I told him, yes, but only the murderer—and that seemed to make him mad for some reason."

"Something tells me this is going to be a long night," I said dismally.

A frenzied whoop from the doorway had me lunging for the thirty-eight again, until my conscious mind caught up with my reflexes. Polly Peridot swayed gently in the doorway, her eyes trying hard to focus. It was patently obvious she had gone to bed loaded. She was wearing a short nightdress that came down only to the base of her stomach, and nothing else. A faded clump of hair showed beneath it.

There was an uneasy silence as the eyeballs belonging to Kempton, Freidel, and myself glazed over. Polly took an uncertain step farther into the room and nearly tripped over her feet.

"What the hell kind of a party is this?" she asked in a heavily-slurred voice.

"Not the kind you imagine, Miss Peridot," Kempton said in a strangled voice. "I imagine!"

"Heard a kind of rumpus and figured it was a party." She gave us a disgruntled and unfocused stare. "Well, the hell with you!"

She slowly shuffled her feet around until she was facing the doorway, and headed toward it in an uncertain swaying kind of intricate dance step, designed to keep her balance come whatever. Somehow, her naked rear view was even more inspiring than her front.

"Disgusting," Kempton said when she was safely out of the room. "Flaunting herself at us like that!"

"I don't know," Dion said dreamily. "She certainly knows what to do with it all."

Maybe things could have still worked out with Lieutenant Schell if I hadn't forgotten to tell him about Kitty and Deborah. It had to be him—who else?—who walked into their room and immediately figured he had discovered a couple more murder victims, or some such. The trouble was that the girls' tempers had built to a point where if they couldn't assassinate Danny Boyd, any other male would do. Still and all, it wasn't smart of me to burst out laughing when I saw them trying to get free.

Schell kept me tied in Santo Bahia for the whole goddamned week, and on the last day he was resorting to lost statements I had to dictate all over again—if and when he could find a stenographer. But even he finally got bored with the game and pointedly suggested I should go burn down the UN building and give New York's finest something to worry about, instead of ruining his life.

I figured the whole thing had not only been a non-profit venture, but also a minor disaster area. It seemed unreasonable to expect Freidel to pay my fee for discovering he was the guy he'd hired me to find, and he was flat broke in any case. Then, out of a rainy gray sky, Harry Kempton appeared at the airport ten minutes before my plane was due to leave. The company would quickly get back onto its feet, he said, now that Reilly and Luman were gone. He'd seen Luman in the hospital where he was being treated for a fractured skull and Art had been glad to sell out his holdings cheap because he was going to need the money to hire a defense counselor the moment he got out of the hospital.

"How about Dion?" I asked.

"He's gone, but it's not important because we'll still have the Freidel label," Kempton said complacently. "There's a brilliant new up-and-coming young designer in San Francisco who's very interested in taking over where Dion left off, so I don't anticipate any problems."

"How about the girls, Kitty and Deborah?"

"They've gone, too. Apparently there was some Hollywood talent scout who was interested in both of them and—"

"I feel sorry for that guy," I said sincerely. "He probably thinks he's taking them for a ride. It sounds like the end of the Freidel dynasty. Where's Dion gone, anyway?"

"He got married."

"I'm glad about that," I said. "At least it's a break for Lenore."

"I heartily agree with you, Mr. Boyd," he said bleakly. "Being legally tied to Dion would have been a disaster for the girl!"

"You mean he didn't marry her?"

"I saw her a couple of days back," Kempton said.

"She told me she'd got a good job with a fashion house in Chicago and was leaving for there the same evening."

"If Dion didn't marry Lenore," I spluttered, "then who in hell did he marry?"

Kempton shuddered. "I still can't shake that ghastly picture from my mind! You remember that dreadful woman shamelessly flaunting her bare buttocks at us?"

I could feel the hysteria slowly expanding inside me. "Polly Peridot?" I could feel my lips curling into a huge grin. "He married Polly?"

"I can only presume," Kempton said distastefully, "that her buttocks talked him into it!"

At the last moment when I was about to board the plane, he suddenly thrust a bulky package into my hands. "I almost forgot, Mr. Boyd. Your fee! I would never have forgiven myself!"

"My fee?" I croaked.

"Double, Reilly said, I remember? The least I could do, you're the man who's put the Freidel company back onto its feet again."

"Double?" I croaked.

"Four thousand dollars, I think that's right?"

"Right." I clutched the package tight in both hands and walked through the gate in a kind of golden haze.

"Mr. Boyd!" I heard Kempton's frantic shout way in back of me. "They'll be worth every cent in about four years from now. That's when I calculate we'll pay our first dividend."

If he wanted to yell gibberish at me, I thought fondly, I didn't mind. Right then, Harry Kempton was the nicest guy in the whole world. Two thousand feet above Santo Bahia I opened up the package and gently shook the contents into my lap. After that I sat very still for a long time. By the time I reached Kennedy airport I'd finally resolved the problem of what to do with four thousand dollars' worth of Freidel company stock. I was going to send it to my old friends, Dion and Polly, as a wedding present.

About a week later, one rainy night when even my view from fifteen floors up on Central Park West was a big black nothing, the doorbell rang. It had to be a creditor, I figured, and wondered if I should pretend I was out. But the doorbell was insistent and I finally figured it would be preferable to placate a creditor, instead of listening to the doorbell ring all goddamned night.

I opened the front door and a muffled figure swept straight past me and into the living room. This must be the newest kind of creditor, I figured; the one who gets his money or just moves right in along with you. By the time I caught up she was standing in the middle of the room, had already removed her hood and was shaking her long black hair into place.

"Well," I said cautiously, "if it isn't my socialite acquaintance, Miss Cathcart!"

"So this is your West Side hovel?" She glanced briefly around the walls then shrugged. "Depressing, isn't it?"

I looked at her blankly for a while, then snapped my fingers. "Got it! What time does your boat leave?"

"Boat?" It was her turn to be cautious.

"But you're leaving for Europe?" I frowned at her. "What else would you be doing on the West Side?"

"The vulgar Mr. Boyd." She sighed gently. "What wild romantic memories to conjure with. The erudite wit—the pre-dinner roll in the hay—the murders, and all that virility. Those were fun days."

"I bought a book this morning," I said, real casual. "It's called *A History of Whores!* Your grandmother gets a whole chapter to herself. Did you know she was drummed out of the union because she refused to pay her dues—insisted on paying in kind."

Her lips tightened as she suppressed a smile. "Where does that door lead over there?"

"The bedroom."

"I'm so glad you have a bedroom, Mr. Boyd!" she said breathlessly. "I was so scared we'd have to make love on the kitchen floor, and I'm sure you have mice."

"Only on Thursday, for lunch," I told her.

"Dion sent you a present, but he insisted I had to deliver it personally."

"I sent him a little something worth four thousand dollars," I said nonchalantly, "if he's not impatient, that is."

"Dion said it was your idea, so you figure it out."

"The present?"

She nodded. "Would you like it now?"

"What have I got to lose?" I said nervously.

She took off her raincoat and if it hadn't been mink-lined she would have gotten a cold. Underneath she was wearing a blue satin bra and a pair of curiously shimmering briefs.

"You like it?" she asked.

"You've got to be kidding!"

"The present, I mean?"

"I don't see it yet."

"The bra is probably confusing," she said in a kindly voice. "I'll take it off."

"There!" She dropped her bra across the back of the nearest chair and turned toward me. "Does that make it easier?"

"I'm not too sure about that," I mumbled. "What is it, a kind of double-barreled gift? I mean, do I get the top half of you now, and the rest at Christmas?"

"I thought your brain was dull in Santo Bahia," she murmured. "I never can tell when I'm lucky! The pants, you brainless Boyd! They're special—feel them."

A nod is as good as a license to a Boyd. I placed my hands firmly on her hips, expecting to feel soft silk crush under my grasp, and went to pull her toward me. She stayed right where she was, while my hands slid off her hips and made a dull rasping sound.

"Chain metal," Libby Cathcart volunteered. "Dion says he cheated a little with some aluminum here and there. It's the one and only Boyd prototype chastity-belt in captivity, he says."

"Now that's what I call being thoughtful when it comes to choosing a gift," I said enthusiastically. "You have to stand up all the time, huh?"

"Dion took care of it." She turned her back toward me and suddenly jackknifed from the waist. There was an insert of transparent while silk right where it needed to be. After a while I realized that horrible thudding sound was only my own heartbeats.

Libby straightened up again and walked toward the bedroom. "We've wasted enough time, Mr. Boyd," she said briskly. "I didn't come here for social advancement, let's get to the lovemaking."

I held her in my arms in an embrace that would have been fiercer, but chain metal doesn't give that much. We kissed, passion mounted into fervor, and then she sprawled wantonly across the bed and smiled up at me invitingly.

"There's just one—uh—small problem," I muttered. "How do you get them off?"

"Dion said that was your problem, remember?" She smiled sweetly up at me.

"Well, how the hell did you get them on in the first place?" I shouted.

"There was a funny kind of zip that just disappeared completely when it was done up. Here, I think?" She ran her hand slowly down her left hip. "Or was it here?" She tried the right hip with the same result.

"Please," I whimpered, "try and remember!"

"It could have been at the back." She rolled over onto her stomach and I got the full impact of that white silk insert. "Can you see anything, Mr. Boyd?"

"Will you stop asking goddamned stupid questions!" I could still hear my voice bouncing off the walls five seconds after I'd stopped speaking.

"Don't be impatient, Mr. Boyd," she purred. "I'm sure you'll solve the problem, one of these nights."

"Where could I get a flamethrower at this time of night?" I wondered out loud.

Her legs started to thrash the bed with a slow impatient beat. "If you don't think you can resolve the problem, Mr. Boyd," she said coldly, "perhaps we could watch television?"

My eyes glazed as I watched the rhythmic bounce of her beautifully taut bottom under the transparent silk, and something snapped—like, *zing!*—inside my head. She let out a startled yelp as I slammed my hands down onto the cheeks of her bottom, and dug my fingers viciously into the thin silk until I had a couple of handfuls of the stuff. Then I ripped savagely, and felt an enormous satisfaction as the silk came away in my hands, and kept on coming away. Somewhere along the line it changed from a pliant material to what seemed like a million tiny metal chains that sprayed everyplace in a tinkling cascade. After a while there didn't seem to be anything left to rip, so I stopped trying. The naked Libby Cathcart rolled over onto her back, screaming with hysterical laughter.

"What's so funny?" I growled. "I found a way, didn't I?"

"It's the only way!" she groaned. "Dion told me that in his letter. He also said if you didn't have it off in under three minutes you weren't the man he figured you were."

"How did I make out?" I asked hopefully.

Her eyebrows rose to a majestic height. "That's one hell of a question to ask, Mr. Boyd," she said icily. "Why you haven't even gotten into bed yet!"